SOUL GUARDIANS SERIES

EVA LENOIR

Reprise
Soul Guardians Series *#1*
Copyright © 2021 Eva LeNoir

This book is licensed for your personal enjoyment only. This book may not be re-sold or given away to other people. If you would like to share this book with another person, please purchase an additional copy for each recipient. If you're reading this book and did not purchase it, or it wasn't purchased for your use only, then please return to your favourite book retailer and purchase your own copy.
Thank you for respecting the hard work of this author.
All rights reserved.
This is a work of fiction. Names, characters, places, brands, media, and incidents are either the product of the authors imagination or are used fictitiously. The author acknowledges the trademark status and trademark owners of various products referred to in this work of fiction, which have been used without permission. The publication/use of these trademarks is not authorised, associated with, or sponsored by the trademark owners.

Reprise/Eva LeNoir
ISBN - 9781984298263

This book is dedicated to you.
To your self-doubts.
To your constant second-guessing.
To your self-inflicted abuse.
I see you and I believe in you.

Bach is an astronomer, discovering the most marvellous stars. Beethoven challenges the universe. I only try to express the soul and the heart of man."

— *Frédéric Chopin*

PROLOGUE

Tonight, I walked off the end of the Santa Monica pier.

I purposefully placed myself in a situation that created a devastating ripple effect, affecting the lives of many and yet, too few for my liking. I know I'm no longer alive, but somehow, I don't feel as though I'm dead. I'm in the middle of the nowhere-in-particular. In the eye of the hurricane or the crater of a dormant volcano. It's quiet, but I know deep down in my gut that the turmoil is just around the bend. This limbo is the story of my life and the reason for my death. I'm always just out of reach of happiness, of fulfillment, but at the same time not completely in the depths of Hell.

I had wanted it all to end, but...nothing had truly begun.

I had wanted to be happy, but...my mind would never allow it.

I had wanted to dive into the darkness, but...I was too afraid of succeeding.

I had wanted to live but...life was just a series of disappointments that I could no longer endure.

So, I created a circumstance where, ultimately, the decision was not my own. The consequences not mine to bear. The guilt...oh the overwhelming guilt, was not mine to carry.

I stopped my medication, I drank, and then I walked off the end of the pier.

But like the story of my life, the epilogue is just as fucked up.

My name is Mara and I'm in Purgatory. Unfortunately, this is not a euphemism. This is the story of my death, and then some.

1

"Do you understand, Mara, why you are here?" It was the third time the old man had asked me that question. All I heard was blah blah blah. I was too distracted by my surroundings to focus on details of conversation. The fact that he creepily resembled a cross between Santa Claus and God himself, was mildly destabilizing but that wasn't the worst of it all. No, what kept my mind wandering to anything except his words, was the decor.

We were sitting in an office of sorts. The walls were bookshelves without a single book inside. It reminded me of an old piano I had once seen, the black and white keys had been removed so they could be restored to their original beauty. I remembered thinking that a soundless instrument was an abomination. These bookshelves were much the same.

The sadness slithered from my chest and radiated out toward my extremities until even my fingers and toes were bathed in a painless agony. Somehow, I had convinced myself that dying would be the sole cure for my ailment. The magic pill against the darkness that controlled my every move, thought, and opinion. I ardently believed crossing over to 'the other side' would lead to a brightly lit tunnel with angelic music guiding my way into immediate happiness. Just one more fuck-up on my long, inexhaustible list of them.

"Mara?" Oh, him again.

"Yes."

"Yes, you understand?"

"Why is everything charcoal gray?" I needed answers before I could continue, I longed for the familiarity of knowledge.

"Why do you think it's charcoal gray, Mara?" His even, calm voice never fluctuated. The pitch annoyingly stable and yet not necessarily monotone. How did he do that? It was painful to my musical ear. My mind was spinning in ten different directions, trying to understand how the sound coming from his mouth could have no variations. By definition, sounds had their own pitch, their own scales. This was insanely unnatural.

"Why are the bookshelves empty? It's a waste of space." And immeasurably sad.

"Why do you think the bookshelves are empty, Mara?" Jesus All-Fucking-Mighty.

"Are you kidding me right now? I didn't die just so I could be analyzed by some after life 'death shrink'. Trust me, I've had my share of the living kind. I don't fucking know why the room is completely gray. I don't know why the bookshelves are devoid of books. I don't know why your desk is completely bare. Why are you sitting there looking like you just stepped out of the freaking Bible and yet wearing a three-piece suit that looks like it cost more money than all the Kardashian's asses put together? Who are you? Are you God?"

I watched the man throughout my tirade. Not a flinch, not a frown, not a single reaction. At that moment, I wished I had my laptop so I could do a thorough web search for his man. Find out everything about him. Cross-reference him with all the Biblical characters I'd heard of throughout my life. But then, I supposed there wasn't a Purgatoryclassified.com for me to actually get these details.

He sat back in his office chair, his mouth adorned with an honest smile, his eyes never leaving mine. "No, Mara. I'm not God. I'm his personal assistant."

It took me a second, but then the burst of laughter

erupted from my mouth and echoed across the empty room. I wasn't amused, I was annoyed.

"You're God's PA? What, do you fetch his coffee and make photocopies for him?" I asked between fits of maniacal giggles.

"Everyone has a personal assistant these days, Mara. Even God needs a second right-hand." There may have been a bit of humor in his voice, but I couldn't be sure.

"Jesus, this is unreal." This is just a ridiculous coma-induced dream, and Sophie, my best and only friend, is sitting next to me blabbering about something or other while my sleeping body is lying on an uncomfortable hospital bed.

Ohmygod, I need to wake up. This gray is driving me crazy.

That thought just made me laugh even harder because who was I kidding? I was already fucking cray-cray, right? That's what everyone used to tell me. Isn't that why I ended up here in the first place?

"No, Mara. My name is Ernest, and I'll be evaluating your exit from Purgatory. Whether you go to the Penthouse or the Basement is up to you. I have to say though, if you keep using the Lord's name in vain, you may end up on the fireman's pole with a one-way ticket down."

His words had a sobering effect, causing my

laughter to die. Silence hung in the air like a cold mist on a winter's morning. "What does that even mean?" I had to shake my head, trying desperately to disperse the fog that had taken permanent residence in my mind.

"Essentially, you are neither here, nor there. This is merely a waiting room before we decide where you belong for the rest of eternity. Whether you take the elevator up or down is entirely your decision. Or more accurately, your evolution throughout your stay will be the deciding factor. Each resident has his or her own suite with the bare necessities. No colors, no sounds, no variations. Only your thoughts upon which to reflect."

Perfect. I had never been able to save myself before, so essentially, I was again destined to fail.

But then, I had already known that.

"Shouldn't this be a cut and dry case? I mean, I caused my own death, right? I understand that my religious knowledge is limited but I'm pretty sure suicide is a big no-no in your world. Why don't you just press the down button and get rid of me? One less sinner on board. Bam. Done. Next!" My arms waved around like a person drowning in a sea of despair. *Oh, Irony, will you ever leave my side?*

"That's not how it works, Mara. If life, or death in this case, were so simple, the human race wouldn't be destroying itself at every turn. We are not convinced that your actions were purely suicidal. Thus, the need to evaluate and judge the facts. All of these books written about our Maker and His history were written by men, therefore they are not always accurate and far from perfect. The Bible, the Koran, the Torah and every other guideline basically tell the same story, but all essentially lack important facts." Chuckling at some internal joke, he shook his head slightly and pinned me with a gaze so intense I couldn't help but flinch. "Only those who come face to face with me can hope to understand, eventually. All others are merely guessing." His words penetrated my confusion, clearing my addled thoughts. Unfortunately, the questions kept adding up.

"My understanding of," I swept my arms around to show the vast expanse of the room and beyond, "all this, was that Purgatory was merely a waiting room for Heaven. I mean, if you were destined to Hell then, I don't know, down you went? No passing Go and no collecting your two hundred dollars." As I said those words, I idly wondered if Ernest, here, even got my reference to the age-old Monopoly game.

Judging by his tentative smile, it seemed God's PA was very well familiar with America's favorite family game.

"Some cases are, indeed, cut and dry, Mara. Suicide, however, never is. We cannot allow a good soul to burn in the depths of fire simply because of its profound suffering. That would put us on the same playing field as Satan, himself. We wouldn't want that, now would we?" His words were coated in jest. Had he just made a joke? Cue in the Twilight Zone theme song and my experience would be complete.

Ernest rose, extended his hand, and smiled, which was more expression than he'd had all throughout the meeting.

"We'll meet again, Mara, but before we do, I need you to reflect. Step inside of yourself and take inventory." With those parting words, he nodded in sign of goodbye and stepped away.

I snorted, a bad habit I'd learned from Sophie when we were younger. I would reflect until the cows came home but it didn't mean I'd get any milk out of it. At least none that wasn't spoilt. But here I was, being given a last chance to search my soul, and as much as I wanted to throw out some type of sarcastic, unhelpful comment, I found myself throwing out an unconvincing "Sure, whatever," as I shrugged my shoulders in near resignation. It wasn't as though I had anything better to do.

Before I had time to rise from my seat and wander around my newfound home, I heard Ernest behind me, addressing me in his hypnotically calm voice, "I want you to write music in your head. Something new. Time here is of no consequence, so I'll just tell you that I'll be back soon. Follow the signs for room twenty-three, that will be your suite." Having made his request, which sounded more like homework than anything else, he smiled again and turned, walking out the door without making the slightest sound.

"Bye bye, then, Mr. God's PA," I muttered, before following him out the door and locating the signs that guided me to my new residence.

Writing music was my only comfort. Thankfully, he didn't ask me to cook dinner.

2

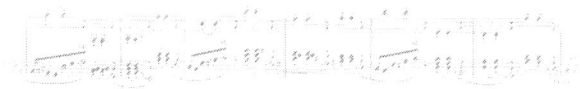

"I can't hear it!" I huffed in exasperation. There was no way of knowing how much time had passed between arriving at my suite and the moment I realized that music wasn't coming to me. Throughout the entirety of my fucked-up childhood, disappointing adolescence, and downright unfulfilling adulthood, music was a constant. My driving force, my hiding place...my ultimate demise. It had been my sanctuary, and now I couldn't hear it. It never occurred to me that with death would come complete silence.

"Maybe I just can't write it." I was reduced to talking to myself since no other sounds accompanied me in this soundproof existence. I decided to try something else. Maybe I could hear music that already existed, that I had learned and memorized. Maybe, I could reproduce.

Sitting on the gray comforter adorned with gray pillows and surrounded by gray walls, I poised my fingers as though a piano sat at their tips. My left hand caressed the invisible white key, my index finger searching the note. My middle finger grazing the black key on a G-sharp, and my thumb pressing the white G.

A-minor.

G-sharp.

G.

Nothing.

Sliding further down, my index summoned the F-sharp before my middle pressed the white F.

F-sharp.

F.

Nada.

Back to the index on the G and the middle on the A.

"No. This cannot be happening." I started over, again and again, only to become frustrated with my lack of success. My music was silent, my world was dead. I couldn't even play Led Zeppelin's 'Stairway to Heaven', that's the accepted default to every musician's fingers, how painfully ironic that it was inaccessible now.

A knock at the door pulled me from my frantic

thoughts. A welcome distraction from the worst possible scenario of my existence.

"Come in!" I called out, guessing it was my Shrink/Judge coming to check on my homework.

"Hey. I just wanted to introduce myself. I live in the suite next door."

Definitely, *not* Ernest. I sat there, on my bed, my fingers poised in mid intro, staring at the man standing at the threshold of my room. I didn't respond, I couldn't.

Without invitation, he walked in and kicked the door closed with the heel of his booted foot before walking up to my bed and making himself comfortable. My eyes followed him as he laid out beside me and propped himself up on his elbows, a wicked, sexy grin lighting up his face. I allowed my gaze to do a quick scan, taking in his attire. Contrary to Ernest, who had been the only other person with whom I'd come into contact, this guy was wearing well-worn jeans that hugged his tapered waist to stunning precision. His torso was covered with a V-neck tee-shirt, revealing strong, capable, and most importantly, inked arms. He wasn't buffed-up but he was solid.

Still, I said nothing.

"My name's Hunter," he started, resting his weight on one elbow and extending his right hand, waiting for me to shake it. "Cat got your tongue?"

I could feel my eyebrows slanting in confusion. "Why are you on my bed?" It was obvious the concept of personal space eluded him. Hunter looked around pointedly before making eye contact with me again, his brow raised on one side questioningly. "I don't see anywhere else I can sit."

"So, you decided that sitting on a stranger's bed was the acceptable alternative?" Although, truth be told, in my living years I would have probably been already making out with him. Physically, he represented the ideal man. Tall, tatted, and with a bad attitude. And by bad, I meant annoyingly forward. With hair cut short, almost shaved completely, and what looked like a perfectly trimmed five o'clock shadow, he seemed too sexy to be dead.

But the eyes.

Hunter's eyes were kind, playful, and soul-searching. I hated them. Hated their chocolate depths that beckoned my deepest, darkest secrets. I didn't like anyone getting too close to my soul and possibly seeing the damaged parts of me that no life or beyond could possibly ever redeem.

"You said to come in...so I did. Thanks, by the way." He winked right before he took his hand away. I never did shake it, nor had I yet told him my name.

"So, you're one of those, huh?" he asked, lying back

with both arms curled under his head as he stared straight up at the gray ceiling. With every movement, the tattoos on his forearms danced like living entities, begging to be noticed. One such tattoo caught my attention. Musical notes wrapped around his bicep, the black ink dancing on his skin like a record player, around and around. What was the song? If I could just lean in closer and sound out those notes…

I tried, and failed, to reproduce the sounds in my head. How frustrating to know the chords but to be incapable of hearing their melody.

"One of what?" My attention landed back to his expressive eyes, immediately narrowing my gaze with my question. If he thought he could just insult me and get away with it, I'd punch him in the balls to prove otherwise.

"The quiet ones. The ones who have so much guilt they feed off it." His gaze never wavered, his voice steady and sure.

It was official. I hated Hunter and his witchy ways.

"And you're one of those, huh?" Two could play the game.

"Ah, here comes the defense mechanism. Go on, Mozart, give it to me."

Arrogant prick. And Mozart? He couldn't possibly know I'm a musician, could he? Regardless, the joke was on him since music had properly written me a "Dear John" letter with a clichéd formula of "It's not you, it's me" in big bold letters.

"The judgy kind," I replied with as much snark as I could muster. "An answer for everything. Must be lonely up there on your high and mighty throne." There. I felt better.

"Nah. I'm just chatty. I like the quiet ones, it allows me to talk more," he answered, matter-of-factly.

I looked over at him and sighed. Maybe a constant voice would be better than deafening silence. "My name's Mara. Everyone calls me...or should I say, called me, Mar." The familiar weight of my ever-present guilt pressed against my chest, making my heart squeeze in phantom pain. Selfishness is a fickle thing. It's obvious in others and yet nearly impossible to decipher when you're the one in possession of it. Sophie and Lucas had given up so much with the hope that one day, all of their efforts and sacrifices would be paid back by a simple, genuine smile on my face. It happened, of course, but they were few and far between and as ephemeral as a butterfly's lifespan. Instead of acknowledging their love and support, what did I do? I took it all away in a moment of self-doubt and anger. No goodbyes, no closure. Nothing but unabashed selfishness. The only positive point was that, now, they could both go on with their lives without having to worry about poor, little Mara and her perpetual eggshells. I usually disregarded my fraying emotions and, technically, I was dead so I couldn't understand why all of my mortal feelings were so constant. So omnipresent. It was disconcerting and I didn't like this vulnerability, not one bit.

Hunter unleashed a smiled that made even the gray walls dissipate into a light so bright it almost blinded me, bringing me back from my momentary self-pity party.

"A beautiful name, for a beautiful woman," he said, sincerity playing from every syllable he spoke.

"Whatever. It was my grandmother's name. She was old and half senile." It was true. I had never assimilated my name to anything beautiful. Wise? Yes. Fiery? Most definitely. Beautiful? Not so much.

"I'm sorry," he murmured, his tone a solemn weight that immediately brought my attention to his captivating chestnut eyes. I stared intently at him only because his gaze shackled me to the spot. I couldn't move, he wouldn't allow it. I could barely breathe from the impact of his attentions.

"Why?" I breathed out.

"You've lost the ability to see beauty, and that, Mara, should be a sin in and of itself."

Normally, I would be flipping him off, hurling

obscenities at him, maybe getting in a couple of well-placed insults regarding his own faults but it all seemed endlessly futile.

"I know. I've been dead a long time," I admitted, if only to stop this conversation from incessantly filling my soul with unwavering darkness.

"Then, wake up and live. Your earthly body is gone, Mara, but your mind? Your soul? They're just on stand-by, waiting for you to open your arms wide and accept the exquisiteness that lies in wait." Using his abs to right himself into a sitting position, he leaned in close, and whispered so softly I barely heard the words. His mouth close to my ear, his breath stroked a line down the outer edge of my lobe and sent a shiver dancing down my spine. "Music exists within beauty. Accept the latter and the former will follow."

In a move so quick I almost missed it, Hunter brushed his soft lips across my jaw before hopping off the bed and disappearing behind the now closed door of my room.

'Music exists within beauty. Accept the latter and the former will follow.'

What did that mean?

Was he talking about the musical notes that had abandoned me inside my mind? My lack of musical inspiration? If so, where the fuck was I supposed to find beauty in a place where gray was the only color available?

From the corner of my eye, I noticed an oval, metal-rimmed mirror hanging on the wall. It blended seamlessly in the identical color scheme, but my own movement had drawn my gaze straight to it. Strange that I hadn't seen it before now.

Slowly, I made my way over and sighed before looking at my own reflection.

Dirty blonde hair, brown eyes, average nose, nondescript lips.

Bland.

That was what I saw. All my life, I had seen my potential but had never reached it. I had felt the greatness within me but had never tapped into it. I had heard my talent reaching out but had never pulled it to the front and center of the stage. No, that was Sophie's specialty.

Sophie, the beautiful.

Sophie, the smart.

Sophie, the natural.

Sophie, Sophie, Sophie.

And me? I merely accompanied her greatness. The brighter she radiated, the dimmer my light became, until one night, it faded completely.

Raising my eyes back up to my reflection, I brought

my index finger to my lips and traced their outline. At least they were symmetrical. Not too plump to mistake them for a Botox project gone wrong. Not so thin that they looked non-existent. As I ran my fingers from my top lip down to the bottom and up again, I decided that they could, in fact, be described as kissable. If every other part of me was disposable, I could at least be honest with myself and admit that my lips had some type of appeal.

There was always that.

3

"Mara, it's nice to see you again. Were you able to make music since last we spoke?" I was back in what I had baptized the 'soulless room' with the man who held such a mortal title, it was perplexing to consider. A personal assistant to God. And here I had been taught that He was all mighty. But when you have an entire world to manage, the task had to be too vast for just one. Funny how my religious beliefs as a living being were minimal, and yet, here I was, vying for a spot in the most sought-after residence beyond death. That wasn't to say that the pits of Hell weren't open wide and awaiting my arrival. I was dead, I wasn't ignorant.

"Mara?"

Shaking my head from my internal thoughts, I was

brought back to the here and now by the soothing, even-toned voice of the man before me. Ernest. The judge, the shrink, the PA.

"Sorry. I...uhm, was thinking..." And so I was back to the present at hand.

"Of course. I understand."

"Right. Well, no. I wasn't able to make music or even hear it for that matter. I don't understand it, I always had too much in my head, and now it's just...gone. It's like it never existed, yet my fingers have their own motor memory. I can move across a mental keyboard but the sounds they would create never come. Why is that? Why can't I hear anything?" I could feel my heartbeat speed up. How was that possible? Did I even have a heart anymore?

"I feel as though my points of reference have been completely obliterated. I don't know who I am anymore." The tightness in my chest was familiar. The overwhelming constrictions that were preambles to my panic attacks. My depression engulfing me in a cloud of despair.

Fuck.

Breathe.

"Breathe, Mara." Ernest's voice echoed my own thoughts, calming me somehow. For once in my miserable life, I didn't feel alone. Surrounded by people and yet completely solitary.

"Breathe..." we both said in unison, and to my utter surprise, it worked. My respiration slowed to a more natural rhythm, my heartbeat even and steady. My mind pushing the dark clouds to the furthest edges of my consciousness.

"Good," he said like a father rewarding his child for a job well done. It was foreign to me, a concept I had difficulty grasping no matter how many times I had wished to gain it. I liked it. That recognition. That pride for a job well done.

I had never been good enough, not in my eyes at least. Maybe not in anyone's. Who knew?

"Let me answer you in progressive steps. First, you must create new points of reference. You must adapt, Mara. That is the single most important lesson you must learn. Observe, learn, adapt. It is the only way of stepping up through the proverbial gates."

"I met Hunter," I blurted out, for no other reason than his soulful eyes flashed through my thoughts.

"I know. I also know you made progress," he said with a knowing smile.

Clearly, Ernest was delusional. What progress? I was still a nonsensical mess, my emotions bouncing off the walls of my mind.

"Really? And where did you get that ridiculous impression?" My tone was childish at best, petulant and sarcastic a more realistic description. With a small flick of his gaze, my eyes were immediately drawn to an item that had most definitely not been there the last time I had sat in this same exact chair.

A book.

A small one but a book, nonetheless. In the vast and numerous rows of empty shelves, this book was certainly the odd man out. "What is that?" I asked, my stare never veering from the lone collection of pages just begging for me to thumb through them. To read. To learn.

"Go on, Mara. Go see what it says." No sooner had the words sounded in the room, I was on my feet heading directly toward the bookshelf. My hands trembled as I inched closer, almost touching what seemed to be a leather cover. It looked old, worn, as though it had been decades since anyone had flipped through the pages. The scent of aging paper enveloped my senses, acting as an immediate balm to my racing thoughts.

The cover had no title, no author name, no accolades. Simply a battered layer of leather summoning me to dive into its story. I succumbed to the urge and exposed the first page. The shock of the words almost had me dropping the book, my gasp echoing around the empty room.

"What...is this?" I asked, my voice a mere whisper.

"Keep reading, Mara."

Taking a deep breath of fortitude, I found the courage to turn the page.

Mara Mona Reece.

'A Brother's Sacrifice'

Oh, Lucas. My brother. My twin.

Staring at my name and the title of this tiny book, I tried to imagine what the rest of the pages would tell me. When had Lucas sacrificed anything for me? In the haze of my depression, I remembered his constant looks toward Sophie. The condescending communication between the two of them, silent questions about my impending breakdowns. Even when I was doing my best to be on top of my oppressive emotions, their worried expressions only made things worse. Made *me* worse. Of course, they thought I was too immersed in my own darkness to notice them, but I did. Unfortunately, I always caught those fucking silent conversations.

"You can take it with you, Mara. Read it, and learn from it. Every word written is a perfect rendition of how things happened," Ernest interrupted my simmering anger, replacing it with confusion.

"How...?"

With an arched brow and a smirk upon his lips, he waited for me to come to my own conclusions.

"Do you have monks sitting around somewhere writing people's lives out by hand? Sounds a bit like forced labor to me." I was trying for humor, something Ernest apparently lacked when it came to the inexplicable possibilities of the afterlife.

"We have scribes. For each soul living on Earth, we have a writer transcribing his or her life. An accurate account of actions, feelings etc..."

"Oh," was all I could say, suddenly feeling as though I should be ashamed for some, maybe all of the things I had done in the past.

"Now," he began, shifting in his seat and taking a more shrink-like demeanor with his long legs gracefully crossed at the knees. Great, just what I needed. "Tell me about Hunter." I took that as my cue to return to my seat facing the bland desk between us, the small book clutched to my chest.

"I don't know, I just ran into him..." I began as I sat my ass down.

"Don't do that, Mara. Do not play emotional mortal games with me. We know all, we see all, and we most definitely feel all. I'll give you a pass on the lying, just this once. Consider that your warning, child."

Inhaling deeply, I closed my eyes before releasing a loud breath, and my sarcasm along with it. I knew it was a defense mechanism, but old habits die hard, apparently. *Pun intended.*

"Okay. Hunter came to my room. He's...well, he's different, I guess. He said something that has been running through my head for a while. He said '*Music exists within beauty. Accept the latter and the former will follow.*' Is that supposed to explain something to me?" I looked up at Ernest with expectant eyes. Suddenly, I felt like a child needing answers that would miraculously give sense to the world around me. Maybe help put things in perspective, so that I didn't always feel like a dying tree in a gigantic forest filled with healthy greens. Everyone here spoke in riddles and I needed some concrete answers. No more, 'You need to figure it out, yourself,' type responses but the honest, 'Go right. Then go left' kind.

That was it.

I needed guidance. For the past however many years this mental cancer had been invading my will to live, I'd needed guidance.

"Yes, it is. How did you feel while you were with him?" Ernest asked, tilting his head to the right, his eyes intent on my face. It didn't escape my notice that he hadn't really answered my question. Such a professional psych thing to do. I had to think about that for a few minutes. Every time my psychiatrists had bombarded me with that same exact question, my skin would prickle, and my anger would boil. Of course, my answers were always the same—'*I feel like committing mass murder then bathing in the blood bath.*' Obviously, that answer never boded well for my mental evaluations. After a while, they recognized it as my way of telling them to fuck off and leave me alone. Not that it ever worked.

"I felt...content, I think. I just, I don't...I mean, the darkness?" I knew I was stammering but I just couldn't get the words out. Thankfully, Ernest came to my rescue.

"There is no place for darkness here, Mara. Only healing. Hunter was drawn to you. Your aches and pains are similar, so his soul was pulled toward your own. Sisters in misery, you could say." A small chuckle escaped the man's lips. He looked as though he were remembering fond snippets of his life and enjoying the mental walk in the park.

"Like...soul mates?" Looking back at me, Ernest smiled and nodded. This was getting a bit weird. Was he trying to set me up? What was this? MatchInHeaven.com? I flushed at the thought, I mean, who wouldn't want to be mating souls with a man like

Hunter? And by "souls", I meant the naughty bits that would land me in Hell.

"That's a very human term, Mara. Here, we talk about sister souls. Our Father feels we all deserve to be bound to another whether on Earth or in the afterlife. Two entities that bond, make for one stronger soul. Down there, Sophie and Jake have bonded. In your mental despair, you missed the beauty of that significant moment. The growing links of their bodies and minds, the necessity of their union."

"Let me stop you right there, Father Kringle. I didn't miss a damn thing. I saw the way they were devouring each other. Indecent, if you ask me." I shrugged my shoulders and shook my head as though the idea of my best friend and her beau getting it on was unpalatable. I supposed it was, in a way. In her quest to please him, she forgot about our music. It became her music for him. It became their symphony, and my instrument was left out in the cold. Silenced.

It became their song, and left me without a trace of a melody.

The happier they became, the darker my thoughts ran.

I hated it. I loathed that I couldn't simply be happy for them. I didn't want to be that person, that insufferable, acidic, toxic, person who couldn't give an inch if she weren't taking a foot.

I wanted to be Lucas, smiling and happy all the time. Playing music without a care in the world. Why couldn't I be his twin in every way?

"Your homework, this time around, is to read your book, and when Hunter comes around to see you, I want you to open your mind. Breathe in his aura and accept his words. Maybe, just maybe, you'll hear music."

I snorted at his words. "You got a magic wand stashed behind that desk, Saint Nick?"

"Child, the sooner you drop your shield, the sooner your fate will be sealed."

With that, Ernest rose from his seat and left me bewildered, my eyes staring at gray nothingness.

The idea of my fate being sealed made that pressure in my chest return. That ache like I didn't have any control over my life. Or death, in this case. And soulmates? That was a thing? Seriously?

No, *not* soulmates.

Sister souls. The pull I had felt toward Hunter earlier...could it have been our souls, one reaching for the other? With only a few words, a pool of hope deep within me had begun to form, something I didn't think I was capable of doing. Shaking my head as though my thoughts were addled in cobwebs, I forced my mind to return to reality. Hope was for the birds, it flapped its wings and took your life along with it. Ernest must have been a romantic, his matchmaking skills in full effect.

But what if he were right?

'Maybe, just maybe, you'll hear music.

4

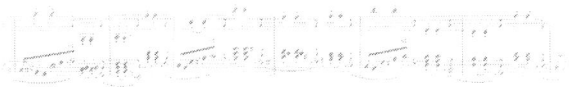

"How did it go, Sassy?"

My head snapped up at the sound of Hunter's baritone voice, humor lining every syllable. Apparently, we were quickly becoming BFFs where showing up uninvited in my sanctuary was the norm. So much for privacy in the afterlife's waiting room. And that nickname? Just, no.

"Sassy? Really? That's the best you could come up with? I sound like a hyperactive teenager with an overly colorful wardrobe." My clothes were as black as my soul, the only color I accepted came in the form of nail polish and lipstick.

Sitting on my bed, legs spread shoulder-width, forearms resting on his knees, Hunter tilted his head in my direction and rewarded me with a smile so captivating my knees threatened to buckle. A quick scan of his body revealed he was dressed in the same clothes as the last time he'd waltz in my suite, his musical tattoo hidden beneath the sleeve of his tee-shirt.

There were more important things on my agenda than flirting and fawning over some guy. Even if his milk chocolate-colored eyes were just as enticing as a box of Valrhona truffles. I fought the urge to throw myself at him. In my defense, I didn't think it was at all appropriate to have carnal thoughts toward a fellow Purgatorian or In-Limbo-ist. It seemed perverse, like doing it in your parents' house when their room was just on the other side of your wall.

I didn't think God would appreciate us getting it on under his roof. Or cloud. Or…whatever the fuck.

From what I had gathered in my earlier conversation with Ernest, everything was somehow monitored by omniscient eyes and ears. Nothing new, really, considering my every breath was scrutinized during my time on Earth. God forbid a sigh would escape my mouth, it would lead Lucas and my parents into a frenzy.

'Is she okay?'
'Did she take her medication?'

'Did you count her pills?'
'How much sleep did she get last night?'

And on and on... Their concern was exhausting, their fear so palpable I could feel my patience waning with every second that passed.

"I like your fire, Mara. It tells me you're not as dead as you think you are. So, yeah, Sassy fits."

Hunter's words awakened something inside me I thought had disappeared years, decades, ago. *Pride.* I did have fire buried somewhere inside me, yet everyone I knew and loved had mistaken that will to live with despair to off myself. This man that I had seen all of twice, could sense it. What did that say about my family?

"Technically, I'm pretty fucking dead, Sherlock," I deadpanned instead of accepting the compliment.

"Truth. But there's dead in Hell and dead 'up There'. Those are two very different definitions." He accentuated his words by pointing his index finger down and then up, and my stupid gaze followed as though I didn't know where those two eternal destinations were located.

"I don't think it's appropriate to joke about being dead. Like really dead." Hypocrisy was apparently my middle name.

"As opposed to half-dead?" The wink did me in. Fuck it.

Making my way to the bed, since it was the only place we could sit, I grinned back at Hunter. A real grin. One that pulled at the corners of my mouth and had my eyes crinkling from its presence. I liked it. It felt almost foreign, but that didn't mean I didn't bask in its warmth.

"Ah, there she is," the man beside me whispered, his thumb tracing the half-moon edges of my lips. "I knew there was a sincere smile in there somewhere. It looks absolutely gorgeous on you." My cheeks burned from the flush I was sure tinted my entire face. My breath catching in my throat, and my belly dancing the Samba, were sure signs of my embarrassment at such a genuine compliment.

"Whatever," was my only response, accompanied by a small roll of my eyes and a tentative smile. There was no bite to it, no effort to deliver my sarcasm with a punch. Hunter chuckled at that, likely choosing to let the subject go.

"What's this?"

"What?" I followed the path of his gaze, landing upon the book that I still had clutched against my chest.

"Oh."

"Oh? Is that the name of this piece of literary genius?" Hunter asked, a smirk drawn at the corner of his mouth. Damn him and that sexy smile. I wanted to poke it and lick it in equal measure.

"No, smartass. It's something to do with my brother, Lucas," I answered, my eyes shifting left then right, the conversation making me uncomfortable.

"Ah. Your first recap on the bookshelf, yeah? It means you made progress." I looked up then, his words sounding wistful, his eyes glowing with what I interpreted as pride. It wasn't an emotion I saw frequently, but enough that I could recognize it. And right there, in the dilatation of Hunter's pupils, I saw he was proud. Of me.

Wait. What progress?

Frowning, I locked my gaze with his and began asking the obvious question, "What are you..."

"What I'm saying is, every time you make emotional progress, you are rewarded with a tale from your life. A glimpse at the things you missed. The preconceived ideas you harbored. The untruths you were certain were your reality. These books are there to enlighten you and help you heal."

Hunter's long fingers came to the side of my face as his thumb brushed along my cheekbone, eyes boring into mine with an intensity that demanded attention. "You are the sole bearer of your own healing. Act wisely and don't let your human personality eclipse the reality that is inside of you, Mara. I can feel it as I'm sure you can feel mine."

I held my breath, afraid of saying or doing the wrong thing, and destroying, what seemed to me, an intimate moment. Hunter leaned in, and every fiber in my body was convinced his lips would make contact.

They never did, at least not where I wished they would. Instead, he placed a chaste kiss to my forehead and patted the book in my hand before standing and walking out the door.

I was dumbfounded for what seemed like an eternity. What was it with these men just up and leaving without any preamble?

When the door closed, I let out a shaky breath, letting my tense shoulders relax in a slouched position.

The book.

Right.

It was time to face my first demons.

∞

Eight years earlier.
Age: 18

Scribe: Eyes of Mil-Ana

Lucas Reece sat in the corner chair, hidden in the shadows, and counting every exhaled breath from his twin sister's mouth.

One hundred and thirty-six.
One hundred and thirty-seven.
Pause.
Hitched breath with a slow winding stutter.
And the process started all over again.
One.
Two.
Three...

When their parents died, just six months prior, everything had fallen further down the rabbit hole. Mara had already been on the emotional edge of a morose cliff, watching the rough waters below with longing in her glassy eyes. Lucas knew this, felt it deep in his gut. As fraternal twins, every emotion she felt echoed within him and tore him apart in the same breath. Now, the pain was tenfold. The feelings of abandonment planting sturdy roots at the base of her very soul. What remained was her pride. On a good day, she would pretend life was bearable. On a bad day? Well, Lucas wanted to rip his own heart out if it meant saving hers.

So, he watched her. He counted her breaths, her pills, her words. He monitored her every step, making sure it wouldn't get closer to the edge of the cliff. If Mara fell, he'd jump after her.

His only lifeline, keeping his otherwise racing mind in check, was Sophie. Her best friend, his girlfriend. But even there, something was missing. From her, from him. From them both. Lucas was lucid enough to know that their relationship wouldn't stand the test of time. At least not as a couple, but he had high hopes for their friendship. Even then, Mara was the common denominator.

Mara was everything.

She needed to fight and get better, and if she were to give up, Lucas would fight in her place.

He never got a chance to grieve their parents' deaths because he was too absorbed with Mara's life. Something had to give so he pushed his own pain aside to make room for his twin sister's agony.

He would save her...or die trying.

Mara stirred in her sleep, bringing his attention back to the task at hand.

Counting her breaths.

A quick glance to the left told him dawn was on its way, which meant he needed to leave her room and continue pretending that he didn't worry. Pretend everything was just fine.

Pretend he wasn't losing, little by little, the other half of his existence.

He just hoped his determination wouldn't be his downfall. Or, God forbid, hers.

5

I slammed the book shut, the noise echoing around the quasi empty room, disturbing the blanket of silence. I knew my tears were streaming down my face, but I ignored them. I wanted to scream, to curse, to hurl myself against every wall in hopes it would stop the misery from enveloping me in its deadly venom. Instead, I sat on my bed, stunned. I took in deep, satisfying breaths, and just let myself feel, for once.

Hunter had told me these books would start the healing process, yet all I felt was devouring darkness staining my very being. I had only read about half the book, and couldn't help but wonder how I could possibly survive the rest.

It was no secret that Lucas had been worried about

me, every day, every hour, but what I hadn't realized until that moment, was the depth of his pain. The responsibility he carried on his shoulders when it came to me.

The sacrifices...

A gut-wrenching cry bounced from the four walls of the room, my mouth wide open, my eyes slammed shut. I reveled in the release of that ever-present pressure always just beneath the skin. Always there, taunting me. Daring me. Pushing me. So, I cried out again.

And again.

And still I screamed. I howled until my throat relaxed and welcomed the release.

Until the fog that seemed omnipresent began to slightly dissipate.

Until the tightness in my stomach seemed to loosen just a fraction.

Until I felt strong arms latch onto to me from behind, cocooning me in their warmth and protection.

That's when I realized I had fallen to my knees, my head tilted to the ceiling, my arms spread out to the side in supplication, my agony evaporating with every shriek that left my open lips.

"Shh...you're okay. Let it out, sweetheart. Let it all out." Even through my emotional tsunami, I recognized the soothing voice that belonged to Hunter. Like a safety net, he caught me before I fell to despair, and for that I was grateful.

"I wasn't his responsibility!" I screeched as loudly as my voice would allow. "I wasn't his burden to bear! FUUUUCK! I didn't deserve him, Hunter. He deserved so much better than me!"

"Shh, let it out," was all he said. Hunter didn't try to agree or disagree, he just allowed me to purge the festering desperation that had permanently settled inside my body and mind.

"Oh no. No, no, no, no... What is happening with him now? Is he...did he...?" The thought sprang at me like a deer in the middle of a dark, abandoned country road. What if my death was too much for him? What if he'd given up?

"Listen to your heart, Mara. What is it telling you?" His voice was strong yet soothing at my ear. A parachute preventing my aching soul from crashing to the ground, allowing a soft landing just outside the surface of my despair.

Letting myself relax in Hunter's tight embrace, I opened myself up to my heart and searched for an answer. Lucas's radiant smile, his outgoing personality, and his laid-back demeanor didn't rhyme with giving up. He was okay, I could feel it. The warmth of his light still shone bright, deep in my soul.

"That he's still down there, living." The relief I felt that my own words rang true, helped to calm my frayed nerves.

"Good. Come on, up you go." With the power in his thighs, Hunter lifted us both from the floor. Positioning himself behind me on the bed, he curled his inked right arm around my waist. On our sides, front to back, our bodies were perfectly aligned. The pressure of his chin resting atop my head was curiously comforting, especially since I couldn't remember a time in my life where cuddling had been a positive thing. I had hated it. Or maybe, I thought I hated it. Maybe...just maybe, it was all about the person and not about me at all, for once.

That's when I heard it.

It came out of nowhere and flitted at the forefront of my brain.

A note.

A musical note came and left, like the fleeting scent of a blossoming rose.

An F sharp as loud as a Sunday church bell, leaving the echo in its wake.

Gone, now, but it was there.

And so, I wept again.

For my brother, for my life, for my death, but mostly for the hope that began budding at the corner of my wounded but healing heart.

6

"You had a breakthrough earlier, Mara. I must admit, I had doubts at first. The boss and I spent many an hour discussing your predicament and the choices you made as a mortal. We've also been reviewing your fateful day." Ernest stopped speaking, leaving the rest of his thought hanging like a well-aged prosciutto in a dark cave.

"Okay. And? Do I pass with flying colors or have I failed the Gates entrance exams?" Without conscious thought, I leaned closer to the non-descript desk, finding myself yearning for a positive answer. Needing reassurance that I hadn't completely fucked up my afterlife, over one drunken mistake. Because, that's what it was, right? A mistake? Or was I that self-absorbed with my miserable existence that I chose to bask in it for the rest of eternity?

"We haven't decided yet. But here is a question for you, Mara. Why did you walk off the end of that pier?"

And there was the crux of the problem. I fell silent, my words and thoughts a jumbled mess running amuck inside my tired brain. While I tried to make sense of that fateful night, I focused on the gentle man's eyes. Their color was never the same, I realized. Depending on the discussion at hand or the emotional level of the conversation, the shade shifted from a warm brown to a troubled green. At that moment, the seriousness of the matter called for the latter. We stared, in silence. The only sound, my heavy breathing, as I tried to push play on the memories of that night.

I was angry. Pissed off that Sophie would betray me. Betray our music. *My* music. We were so close to making it, so close to having everything we ever wanted, but Sophie, she backtracked. Maybe it was fear or maybe it was pride, but whatever it was, it ended with a single flick of her thumb. Years of work, of late nights at the piano scratching out D-minors to replace them with E-flats. Of balling up entire sheets of music paper and throwing them in the waste basket only to start all over again. Thousands of hours spent creating and fine-tuning the perfect sound, the hook in the melody that would bring the public to tears. We had that, and in fit of rage, she watched them turn from art to ashes in the middle of our chimney.

Or was it my rage? She didn't want to sell out to the big wigs, our music was too important to hand over to just anyone throwing a few hundred bills our way. I wanted the recognition. I wanted to finally feel like someone heard me. Sophie's voice was impossible to ignore, she could enthrall her audience without a single sound to accompany her. Next to her, I was nothing. Non-existent. Inconsequential.

Sophie was the opus where I was a mere jingle. Catchy but meaningless.

That night, as I drowned my anger in cheap whiskey and fired up my indignation, I couldn't see reason. Hell, I didn't want anything to do with it. My reasoning was simple: Sophie ruined us, and I just didn't give a fuck anymore. But purposely off myself? No. Yes. Maybe.

"I don't know," I answered truthfully. I could have lied and tried to argue my mental state, but what was the use when Ernest knew, better than I, that uncertainty was my enemy.

"Did you hear music, Mara?" The sudden change of subject threw me for a loop, but once my brain caught up to the conversation, my lips tilted upwards, and I could feel the smile all the way up to my eyes.

"God, yes!"

Ernest frowned at my words, silently scolding me.

"Sorry," I quickly added, feeling admonished.

"Go on, tell me what happened."

"I read Lucas's story which made me cry like a baby. But then, Hunter was there. He held me without judgment or concern that I would have a complete breakdown. He just...he held me, you know? I felt safe for the first time in...ever, I think." I could feel the tears burning, trying desperately to overflow onto my cheeks. I didn't have it in me to hold them back, so with a breathless sigh, I set them free. "I mean, Sophie was my best friend. She was always there for me. She would hold me and rock me and sing to me but...her every action betrayed her fear of my next move. Not Hunter. He just wrapped me up in his arms and let me purge my emotions. It was...nice. Great, even." I felt the veracity of every one of my words, deep in my bones.

Ernest smiled, and with a slight upturn of his chin, he directed my attention to the bookshelves. Sitting alone, engulfed in the empty space, sat a decent sized book. I rose to my feet, pulled like a magnet to the right-hand corner of the room, my feet on autopilot. As I neared the wooden structure, I zeroed in on the book. The cover was some type of leather with gold trimmings. The contrast in color was a visual gift.

Slowly, I raised my hand and ran my fingers along the spine, reading the title out loud.

'Unconditional Everything'

Almost out of fear, I turned to look at Ernest for reassurance, but he was gone.

Alone, I pulled my shoulders back and took a deep, fortifying breath.

'I can do this.' My new mantra.

Slowly, I pressed my fingers around the book and pulled it out of its space.

My forearm swiped the front cover, clearing some invisible dust as though I were an archeologist discovering the original edition of the Bible. Needless action when the cover was pristine, as was the entire room. Or Purgatory for that matter. Not a fleck of dirt or dust.

When I opened the cover, my eyes landed on the first page, ripping a gasp from my already sore throat.

"Lucas and Mara were the reason they loved life. The first thought as they woke, their last as they fell asleep. Every plan, every project, and every word were with their children in mind. A love so unconditional it radiated around them in a bright aura of perfection."

"Jesus...shit...I mean," I looked around as though God himself would sweep down and put me in the corner where I would recite 'I will not take the Lord's name in vain,' a hundred times. "Sorry," I finally said to the empty room, before returning my attention back to the book.

Patrick Reese held his baby girl like a treasure worth all the millions the world had to offer. Bringing the infant to his eye level, he rained soft kisses across the baby's wrinkled skin and branded his instant and unwavering love all over the child.

'I will love you more than life and protect you with every bone in my body.'

Closing the book, I turned on my heel and walked out of the library. I needed the comfort of my own room. Or maybe I needed the possibility of having Hunter catch me when the fall would inevitably come.

Practically running, I quickly made my way to room twenty-three, flopping down on the mattress, and laying on my stomach with my elbows propped up. It was my parents' story, and yet I felt as though I were more detached than for Lucas. And maybe I was. They were ripped out of my life so early, and more importantly, I leaned on Lucas for everything. He undeniably took on the role of my protector, despite my protests that I could without a doubt take care of myself.

Past events showed that I could not, in fact, be entrusted with my own safety.

I felt him before I even heard him.

Hunter.

Without a word, he spread his entire length along the bed and folded his arms behind his head, keeping his eyes closed. I smiled at how naturally he had invaded my life.

"Tell me a story, Sassy."

Ugh. We needed to do something about that fucking nickname.

And so, I did. But not before I turned my body perpendicular to his, resting my head on his stomach with the book held out in front of me. Not the most comfortable position, but one that gave me comfort, nonetheless. Not only could I feel his warmth, but every one of his breaths rocked me like a drifting boat out on the sea. Lulling me into safety and prepping me for a story that almost felt as though it were fiction.

But it wasn't. As I would soon find out.

7

T*welve years earlier.*
Age: 14.
Scribe: Eye of the Rose

Patrick and Suzanne Reese sat at the dinner table, their two teenage children bickering about wanting their independence. Mara wanted her own friends, tired of sharing friendships for the sole reason of being a twin. Lucas had responded calmly, almost jokingly, "Well, stop stealing my friends then and we'll be golden."

With a sigh, Patrick placed his hand on Mara's fist resting dangerously on the tablecloth.

"Sweetheart, eat. We'll sort this out after dinner. Now is not the time." The raised voices suddenly went *mute, but the death glares continued. Suzanne knew that they couldn't win all of the battles, but they were adamant about winning the war.*

"How's school going? Any tests coming up?" Patrick asked Lucas as he scooped up a large fork full of linguini. With a shrug, his growing son finished chewing before giving him a proper response.

"It's fine, I guess. We have a History test next week, but I should be good. Just need to reread the last two chapters on the American Revolution." Patrick nodded, pointing the fork at his son. "Don't wait until the last minute to do that. You want your information to make it to your long term—"

"Long term memory and not fall into short term," they all echoed his long-time mantra when it came to studying. The table fell into laughter as everyone resumed their meals.

"Mara baby, anything coming up for you?" School work wasn't her forte, but music was etched in her very soul. By now, Patrick had learned that if he wanted to have her talking up a storm, it was the subject of music he needed to broach, not English Lit.

"There's a recital on Friday, but I'm not ready."

"Why do you say that?" Patrick knew better than to contradict her. When it came to the piano, Mara never saw the perfection that was her talent. She would

practice until her fingers were raw, until her mind ate, drank, and breathed the partition laid out before her eyes. Half the time, his daughter wasn't even aware of the fact she was humming the notes while doing odd things around the house or riding in the car. An artist's mind in constant limbo between reality and abstraction. A perfectionist was always shy of her expectations and feeling as though she were tumbling into failure on a daily basis.

He should have seen the signs early on. Those warning lights signaling her mind's dangerous dance with depression. They both, as parents, should have done something sooner. The truth was, she was their little princess. The apple to daddy's eye, and the pride permanently living in their hearts.

With all the love they had for her, ultimately, they failed her. The mental professionals tried to balance out her moods, but the medication was never quite doing its job, instead pulling their little girl further and further from her true self.

"Something isn't right, and I can't find it. I thought it was the arpeggio at first. That maybe the sequence was too slow, but when I tried to fix that, the fermata was too long and threw everything else off. I can't find the problem." Her voice was rising with every word, alerting him that maybe this wasn't the subject they *needed to focus on at the table. Patrick's eyes darted over to his wife, a silent communication they had perfected months into Mara's "episodes". Even Lucas had picked up on their codes.*

"Hey, did you meet that new girl? Sophie?" Lowering his eyes to his plate, Patrick breathed a sigh of relief at their son's acute knowledge of his twin sister. She would be okay as long as he stood by her side. They had to believe that.

"Yeah, she's a singer. Her voice needs a little push, though." Mara paused to drink from her water glass before continuing her observation of this Sophie. "But, she kinda sounds like Ella Fitzgerald mixed in with Amy Winehouse. It's hot." Patrick blinked, trying to understand if the word "hot" had taken a different significance since last he used it.

"She's definitely hot..." Lucas muttered, probably hoping no one had heard him. They all did. And just like that, laughter spilled throughout the room and levity filled their hearts. "Oh, and she plays the Theremin which means she's original. I like her." The excitement in Mara's voice returned, acting as a balm to his frantic nerves.

"What is that?" Patrick asked, as he broke a piece of bread to wipe away the white sauce from his pasta plate.

"It's a Russian made instrument. It has, like, two antennas. One controls the volume and the other the pitch. And the really cool thing about it, is that the thereminist doesn't touch the instrument. It's like man and machine are communicating through musical vibrations. So cool."

In that instant, Patrick felt as though Mara were a happy, normal teenager enjoying all the beauty life had to offer.

It's all they had ever wanted. For their children to be happy, to be themselves. To be free of tormenting inner demons.

But sometimes, wishes just can't come true.

∞

"What are you thinking?" Hunter asked, still in the same position as when I had started reading. On his back, arms folded behind his head, and his eyes closed in a semblance of sleep. He was beautiful. Strong features that begged to be drawn or painted; Hunter was an artist's wet dream. Everything about him was a contrast to light and dark. His skin was surprisingly pale, blending his short, dark hair and soulful brown eyes into an intense work of art. And his tattoos. Color upon color dancing across his skin like a story begging to be told. Until that moment, I hadn't realized a man could be described as beautiful. He wasn't the still life beauty of a Renaissance portrait, definitely not the distorted ambiguity of Cubism. No, Hunter was the tangible reassurance of Realism. He didn't embellish like Impressionism, and avoided the mind-games of Surrealism. He was there, and he was real.

"What happened to you? I mean, why are you here?" I blurted out, uncaring that maybe he wasn't one to share his inner battles.

"I died, Mara. Just like you, just like everyone else, here." His voice didn't hold any annoyance, he spoke the truth without apparent regret. How was that possible?

"But, you're so young."

"We're the same age, human wise." He still hadn't opened his eyes, our conversation easier for me when I didn't have to confront the wise irises of his gaze.

"I didn't know that..." I mumbled, but wasn't quite ready to give up on my search for more information.

"How did you die?" I asked, fearing he wouldn't answer. It took a while, but he finally gave me a little piece of his past.

"Fell asleep at the wheel. Crashed into a tree and found myself here." I wasn't sure, but I thought I'd heard the sound of guilt enveloping his words.

"Were you alone?" I barely whispered the question, afraid of the answer. Yet, I knew in my heart that if he'd been alone, Purgatory would be a moot point. Either he had been a decent human and gone off to the Gates or he'd been a horrible person which meant Satan would have been welcoming him with champagne and fiery appetizers.

"No. I wasn't," was all he gave me as a response, effectively putting an end to the conversation.

"Oh."

"Yeah."

It was time to change the subject. I knew this because his breathing had accelerated, the movements of his stomach beneath my head reminded me more of a brewing storm on the sea than a peaceful lulling on a lake. Something told me that Hunter's inner storms were not a force to be ignored.

"My parents deserved better."

I turned my head to look over at him again. His eyes were open, his gaze fixing me like a predator.

"I mean, all they ever wanted was a happy family. Talk about drawing the short straw. It's almost a good thing they weren't around for my demise." They said it wasn't natural to have to bury your own child. So, maybe losing them before I lost myself, was the better outcome to the story. Either way, tragedy was a given.

Hunter was up with lightning quick speed, suddenly pinning me to the bed with his entire length hovering on top of me. I had no idea how I had ended up on my back with his thighs trapping my own. I didn't have time to register his movements before his hands wrapped around my wrists, hiking them up above my head. For a few moments we just stared at each other. My doe-in-the-headlights gaze a stark contrast to his death glare. I was prey and he was clearly the predator.

The hunter.

How fitting.

"Every time you push yourself into the ground with your demeaning words, you are insulting every single person who ever loved you, Mara. Every time you dismiss your worth, you're mocking every effort they ever made to help you. And every time you degrade your mind and body, you are killing yourself a little more. It makes me angry, Mara. Because that means that all of my efforts were for naught." He had barely finished his sentence before the plump cushions of his lips descended upon mine and he literally took my breath away with his mouth. His lower body grinding at the V between my legs. Our chests dancing their own version of a sensual tango. But his tongue. Oh, his tongue owned me. It explored every inch of my mouth. Running over my teeth before he pulled back and nipped my lower lip.

As our mouths separated, Hunter pushed himself up on the palms of his hands and just stared at me.

"You'll be the death of me, Mara Mona Reese."

And then he was gone.

I blinked away the shock of the last few minutes, lifting myself up on my elbows and shaking my head.

What the hell just happened? And why was he so damn angry?

Apparently, Purgatory was just as confusing as being on Earth.

8

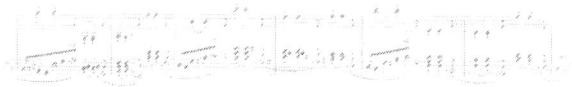

There's nothing more destabilizing than the absolute lack of passing time. Since my arrival in Purgatory, I was incapable of guessing the hour. Or if it was day or night, for that matter. Hunger had evaded me, but as I lay there on my lifeless bed surrounded by the ever-present grayness of the room, I wondered if my body still needed sustenance, or if the stress of the past however many hours or days had simply taken a temporary leave of absence.

With my parents' book resting against my chest as I stared at the ceiling, I couldn't help drifting off to earlier when Hunter had practically attacked and devoured my mouth. It was the most erotic of kisses, a simple testament to endless future possibilities. It didn't escape me that with every further thought of Hunter, my panties grew increasingly wet. The steady buzzing between my legs was monopolizing my thoughts, making it impossible for me to ignore the need. Closing my eyes, I let the back of my hand wander, gliding smoothly over one breast with a feather light touch. Behind my closed lids, all I could see were Hunter's deep brown eyes piercing straight into my soul. In my erotic dreams, he was whispering dirty words to me. Commanding my every movement with the mere tone of his voice. My hand continued its sensual journey beyond the flat surface of my stomach and stopped at the apex of my pussy. I was at a crossroads. I mean, here I was in Purgatory where eyes and ears were apparently everywhere, and I was about to give them an X-rated rendition of Basic Instinct. Never as a living woman had I hesitated in pleasuring myself. It was part of human nature and I refused to feel ashamed for it. But here? Now? With God somewhere probably trying to put world peace into effect? I just couldn't do it. I let my hand drop to the mattress and heaved a sigh of frustration.

Time may not have been passing, and hunger was definitely not gnawing at me, but sexual frustration was alive and well. As my thoughts jumped from one topic to another, I absentmindedly braided my thick blonde hair, reproducing the same movements I had perfected when living with Sophie. Those intimate moments shared between best friends, sisters, really, were privileged. Our girl time without face to face conversations. Fleeting moments where we bared our emotions, our fears, and the thriving hunger to make it in the business. The repetitive actions of crossing strands of hair one over the other had the ability of calming my racing thoughts. It was bliss and torture in equal parts.

A soft knock at my door was a kickstart to my heart, the anticipation of seeing Hunter again brought the teenage schoolgirl out in me.

I knew it was Hunter, who else could it be?

"Yeah? Come in," I managed to say as calmly as possible.

The door slowly opened, and like a vision from my self-induced porn film, Hunter stood at the threshold, studying me.

"What's wrong?" he asked, his voice tight, bordering on edgy.

"Uh, nothing. I was just...uh...braiding my hair? Maybe even dozing off."

"Why are your cheeks flushed?"

And that was a fantastic question to which I had no answer. At least, none I wanted to give to him.

"Did you need something?" I asked, hoping the

change in subject would distract him from my appearance.

"Nope," he answered, popping the 'p' and pushing off the door jamb, making his way slowly toward me. "Just wanted to check in. Make sure you're doing okay." He was close. Too close.

"Well, well, well. What might we have here, Hunter?"

And for the second time in little to no time, I felt my heartbeat speed into overdrive at the disruption. A rich, baritone voice echoed off the walls, as a newfound stranger casually peered inside my room.

The sound that came deep from Hunter's throat was not human. It was feral, like a trapped animal warning its assailant of his imminent attack. My eyes were automatically drawn to the figure standing at the exact spot Hunter had occupied only moments earlier. Except this man had nothing in common with my Hunter. Actually, that wasn't completely accurate. The predatory stare that graced the man's face was the exact same as the lust filled eyes Hunter had directed my way more than once, already. Trouble was, this man scared the fuck out of me. Something so dark and dangerous emanated from every pore, a luring smile paired with death at every turn.

With his jet-black hair slicked back Sinatra-style,

and his black irises lingering on every inch of my body, I felt invaded and mentally raped from his look alone. A shiver ran straight down my spine, which had no similitude to the one I had experienced when Hunter's mouth had been worshipping me with every lick and bite. No, this shiver did not bode well.

"What the fuck are you doing here, Samael?"

Why was it that in a world of gray, this man had the privilege of color? The dark suit he wore was accented by a blood-red dress shirt, the buttons at the top left undone, giving him a Godfather allure. Topped with a red hankie carefully tucked inside the breast pocket of his suit jacket, this man looked as though he owned nightclubs. Or brothels. Samael, as Hunter had called him, looked and felt like pure, unadulterated sin right down to the timber of his voice.

"Such language for a pure soul, Hunter. I'm a little disappointed, if not hopeful, you might take a trip down to my humble abode." Samael turned his scrutiny back to me, as a slow, sensual grin made his face that much more attractive. Lethally, so. I may have died young, but in my twenty-six years on Earth, I'd seen that look more times than I'd care to explain. This man had hunger written all over his face and he was making zero effort to hide it. Not from me, and certainly not from Hunter.

As if on cue, Hunter stepped in front of me, hiding me from Samael and his wandering gaze.

"Shame. I was enjoying the view. But no matter. It's time, Hunter. We have a meeting, and you know how the Higher-ups despise tardiness." Samael leaned to the side so as to direct his next words directly to me. "It was an immense pleasure to finally meet you, Mara. I have no doubts we shall meet again. Hopefully, it will be more at my advantage next time around." Winking at Hunter, a sure message of taunt, Samael turned on his heel, and started walking back out as he spoke over his shoulder. "Your presence is needed, Hunter. *Now*."

Once the man was gone, Hunter turned to me with worry etched on his face. "Stay here, okay? Don't move, and wait for me to get back." After a few moments of us just staring at each other, Hunter placed both palms over my cheeks and leaned down, brushing his soft, delectable lips over mine. Just a whisper of flesh against flesh. A message meant just for me. A plea, really. Closing my eyes, I reveled in the feel of such mortal contentment, something so human in a place that was anything but. "I'll be back," he repeated as he drew away from me and took a step back. I nodded, not knowing what else to do. I mean, where was I supposed to go, anyway?

"Okay." I didn't know why I suddenly felt the urge

to whisper, but that was how my one-word answer came out.

I waited for Hunter's return like a woman waits for her soldier coming home from war. Except he wasn't a soldier, and I wasn't his wife. Or even his girlfriend, for that matter. I was his neighbor in the Limbo Motel where the owners hadn't even bothered with the little mints on the pillows. In fact, there were no more wars either, and death was already all around us. None of my references made any sense. From the moment I jumped off that pier, the concept of normality was but a mere figment of my prior knowledge.

I found myself in Purgatory. I learned God had a PA who looked more like Santa Claus than a secretary, and apparently souls could find each other in the drab waiting room to the afterlife. It all sounded a little too close to fate and destiny. Like our lives and paths were all written out, and we were basically manipulated puppets with only free will to guide us. I'd never bought into that story. But now?

Was this my destiny? Finding love beyond the realm of the living?

Just my luck. Mara Reeves found the hope of love as her mortal body rotted somewhere in the belly of Los Angeles. The City of Angels. How fucking ironic is that shit?

9

As always, time had no meaning in Purgatory. Minutes, hours, days, months...they were just blurs of space between conscious moments. I was asleep when Hunter returned, waking me as he slid in behind me on the bed. Warm breaths caressed my neck, one arm snaking under my head replacing the pillow, as the other wrapped around my own across my chest. Lacing his fingers with mine, he whispered through the silence. "Hey, beautiful." He knew I had awakened to his movements, but I kept silent. I needed some answers, but I wasn't certain he had them. Before I could conduct the next Inquisition, I had to get my mind straight. Be direct with my inquiries.

"Just ask, Mara."

"Who was he?" I blurted out.

"Samael?" he asked, avoiding it seemed.

"Yes."

"Be careful what you ask for, Mara. You cannot 'unknow', and sometimes information is best kept in Pandora's Box."

Fuck, I always hated riddles.

"Hunter, please. Just answer my question. What am I going to do, have a mental breakdown?" A sarcastic laugh escaped through my mouth. "Been there. Done that." Behind me, Hunter stiffened for a mere second but long enough for me to feel it. Whether it was fear, anger, or surprise at my words I would never know but he did have a definite reaction.

"You were confused, Mara. It's not the same thing."

Ah, yes. The synonyms.

About six months before going for a midnight swim loaded with an abundant amount of alcohol in my system, I had made a list. It was meant to amuse me but had, in fact, pissed me off more than anything.

The title was still so fresh in my mind: "Socially Acceptable Ways of Naming Depression." It had become a game for me, because it was common knowledge that the "D" word was not to be used.

1. Sick
2. Ill
3. Tired

It's not depressing if it sounds like a flu.

4. Under the weather
5. Hurting
6. Irritable

It's not depressing if it sounds like PMS.

7. Sad
8. Exhausted
9. Preoccupied

It's not depressing if it sounds like a grieving episode.

The truth of the matter is that my depression was not a moment. It was part of my life. As music was my oxygen, my highs and lows served as the carbon dioxide I exhaled with each breath. I had learned to accept it, to live with it and to hate it with every fiber of my being. My family? Sophie? Well, they never could accept it, so they fought it and ultimately lost to their fears.

We all lost...but then life was a gamble, our very souls the bargaining chips.

"What are you thinking about, Sassy?" I heard Hunter ask from behind, pulling me back to the task at hand.

"About life. Or lack thereof." I chuckled but could tell Hunter was not amused.

10. Confused

And the list goes on.

"So, who was he?"

"His name is Samael."

"Don't do that," I said, turning around to face him. Needing him to know that I wasn't a child to be handled with condescending care.

"Don't do what, Sassy?" he asked on a murmur.

"Treat me like a five-year-old. I know his name. I want to know who he is. Why was he wearing colors? Why did he come off as an asshole? Why was he looking at me like he wanted to devour me?" That last question got Hunter's full attention. He sighed, turned to lie on his back, and brought my head to his shoulder, cradling me in his protective hold.

"He's the Angel of Death, Mara. Equal parts good and evil. The leader of Fifth Heaven with two million angels working under him."

Sitting up straight, I looked Hunter straight in the eyes and tried not to tremble from his words. I failed, obviously.

"Satan?" That made no sense.

It was Hunter's turn to chuckle for some crazy reason.

"Sorry. I'm not mocking you, Mara. It's just that he hates being confused with Shaytan. Apparently, he feels he's too good looking for what that name implies."

I knew I was staring but...*fuck*.

This was surreal.

"So, if he's not Satan then...who is he? I don't get it, Hunter. He said he was hoping it would all end to his advantage." What the actual fuck was going on? At that moment, I wished I had researched religion more thoroughly, but my mind had always been overly consumed by facts of those who could help my career, my craft, my music. Religion was just something going on in the world, having no bearing on my art.

With an arm under his head, and a hand slowly stroking the blonde strands of my hair, Hunter went into storytelling mode. Knowing answers were about to be handed to me, I relaxed in his embrace and listened to the soothing melody of his voice.

"There are many renditions of what has happened and is still happening in God's Kingdom. The first thing you need to understand is that religions are a man-made phenomenon. They are all correct and yet are all wrong at the same time. In fact," he added, kissing the top of my head before resuming his tale, "they are all one and the same."

Closing my eyes, I recalled some of the earthly events concerning wars on religion. Catholics fighting Protestants. Muslims fighting Jews. Everyone fighting everyone in the name of their Maker.

"The Ten Commandments were written by men. The prayers were created by poets. The multitude of rules were a human fabrication. Father never asked for any of it."

"But..." I knew there was something missing, but I just couldn't think of a question more important than another.

"Mara, the only thing He ever wanted, was for his children to love each other. We failed so, in turn, he feels he has failed. Everything just escalated into all of these ridiculous sins." Hunter's voice had taken a defeated note causing me to raise my head, looking him straight in the eyes.

"How do you know all of this? How long have you been in Purgatory? I mean, I don't know any of this."

Lifting himself up to a sitting position, Hunter swung his legs to the side of the bed, bowed his head, and rubbed the short remnants of his dark hair. Sighing, he took a minute before speaking again; his back to me as I kneeled on the bed, confused.

"Hunter?"

"Look, Mara. There are things I cannot tell you, yet. Before you can have knowledge, you need to heal. You have to find yourself before finding the truth." With that, he rose to his feet, turned to face me, and placed a chaste kiss on the top of my head.

"I need to go. Read your parents' book, answers will surely be there for you."

"But Hunter...I don't..." Understand? Want you to leave? Fucking have a clue what's going on?

All should have been questions I could have hurdled at him, yet my throat closed up and words evaporated through the fog of my confusion. Once again, I found myself alone. In silence. No words to comfort me, no music to protect me. No lyrics to inspire me. Solitude wasn't just the story of my life, it was apparently the story of my death, as well.

From the corner of my eye, the simple cover of my book called to me. Urging me to do as Hunter asked. Encouraging me to look beyond my fear and self-hatred, and learning to open my emotional horizons.

So, that was what I did.

I read.

I wept.

I learned.

All the while, I broke just a little more.

10

Hunter had stopped by after I'd woken from a restless sleep. He'd come to tell me about his meeting with our resident PA, and that he would be back shortly thereafter. Leaving me with a heart-stopping grin, he had winked at me just as the door fully separated us from view. My sigh at his boyish gesture had been worthy of a Sweet Valley High chapter. Pre-death Mara would have heaved at the excess sweetness in the whole scene. Post-death Mara was soaking it up.

Perched upon the bed, I absently stared at the gray wall facing me, thinking of everything yet nothing in particular. I was desperately searching for notes, for music to fill the empty spaces of my head, but I heard nothing. I felt nothing. One of my hands instinctively reached up to my long blonde hair and trapped the strands between my fingers, sliding them to one side over my shoulder, as I had done thousands of times before while living with Sophie. I began braiding intricate patterns. Once I reached the ends, I started the process all over again. As they had in the past, these mindless actions helped my mind to focus on what needed to be done or said. It was never about creating the perfect braid, but more about occupying my fingers and hands so my thoughts could concentrate on more important details in my life.

Unbraiding my hair, I started over again, seeking insight.

Why had I been so unhappy, then?

Was it the obvious death of my parents? I didn't fully accept this reasoning because I knew my darkness had started well before then. Their accident was merely the catalyst that brought the axe down.

Was it my uncontrollable craving for perfection? I couldn't reconcile with that notion. Seeking out the most flawless strings of notes should not have been a plight but a sublime journey.

Was it my competitive nature? In music, where my obsession for being discovered ruled over a large portion of my days. In my role as a twin, where being unique seemed unattainable. In friendship, where my jealousy for Sophie grew exponentially with every note that she sang to the crowds drawn to her like sailors to a pin-up goddess.

As my fingers twisted the last available strands, the terrifying thought that every single one of my "quirks" were, in the end, my downfall. I did nothing in half-measures. I did everything with my entire being, even on that fateful night when instead of kicking my feet up to reach the surface of the water, I let the abyss drag me down. I kept my eyes open and watched the lights fade as my body slowly fell to the bottom of the ocean. Of course, the alcohol had been to blame for my initial desire to jump off the pier, but my inability to kick my feet upward was my very soul giving up. I knew it then, and it was blaringly clear as I sat there introspecting just as Hunter had asked me to do.

I was to blame.

I was a sinner.

I had no business being in Heaven, committing suicide was a guaranteed way of getting a one-way ticket to Satan's lair. I supposed I deserved it.

Would I ever see Hunter again once I pushed the down button on the elevator to Hell?

Obviously, I didn't wish for his fate to mirror mine, but the thought of spending eternity separated throughout our entire existence was like a boulder pressing forcibly against my sternum.

I could lie. Tell them I hadn't meant to kill myself. Explain that I was hot and needed to breathe.

Even as I contemplated that option, I knew it was fruitless. I was sure they already knew the answer and were just waiting on me to come to the same conclusion.

With determination in my gut and a steel rod in my spine, I rose to my feet and lifted my chin.

It was time to face my sins.

11

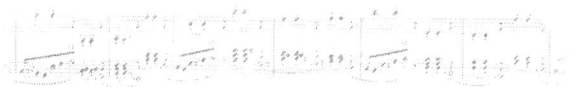

My big girl panties firmly in place, I let my hair drop down over my right breast and took the first steps toward my destiny. The doorknob felt cold and unrelenting under my touch, but I turned it nonetheless, walking out of my gray confines and heading to the room where my conversations with Ernest took place on a regular basis. Slowly, I made my way down the morose hallway, focused on my destination, when I heard the faint sounds of bliss. A repetitive onslaught of G-minors. The fingers on my right hand itched to drum it out against my thigh. Without thought, I gave in to the temptation, let the comfort of finally hearing music guide my tempo.

In my mind, each press of my thumb, index, and pinky respectively landed on B flat, D, and G. The notes danced on my thigh, counting out the triplets that guided the singer's sultry voice. That's when it finally dawned on me.

'Feeling Good' by Nina Simone drifted through my mind, spreading a large smile across my lips as my entire being realized I could hear music again. My left hand joined in with a slower, more seductive rhythm of octaves playing along my other leg. I could practically taste the melody, smell the ivory keys of my piano. My body abuzz with a high so familiar I almost missed the sounds of an argument.

The voices yelled in hushed tones. My feet stopped before I turned the corner, hiding myself from view as I unabashedly eavesdropped a conversation that, clearly, wasn't meant for my ears.

"You're a bastard, you know that?" I recognized the baritone of my Hunter. The anger was palpable enough that I could feel it running down my own spine.

"You're one to talk, kid." Who was that? I tried to remember why the voice sounded so familiar when it finally hit me.

Samael.

I knew something was off with him. I gave zero fucks to the fact that I was listening to a conversation that I shouldn't have been privy to.

"Stop calling me that. It's condescending, and

considering your job, well...I'd shut my fucking mouth if I were you." Hunter was pissed off, and I was dying to know why. No pun intended.

"Look, you needed me to do it. I'm not usually a giving guy but what can I say? You've grown on me." Samael's tone didn't sound angry in the least. He was as calm as he had been the one time I had met him.

"You had no right. She wasn't ready, it wasn't her time. Fuck, Sam, what if I can't fix this?" Hunter no longer sounded livid but had unexpected sorrow lining each of his words. Was he talking about me?

"Fate, Hunter, is just another word for my job. Thank me, and we'll carry on." A fraction of a second later, I heard the distinct sound of a fist hitting unyielding matter.

"I can't fucking carry on, Sam. What. If. I. Can't. Fix. This? What the fuck do I do then, huh? Did you ever think of that before you had her walking off that fucking pier?" By that time, Hunter was spitting his words, the ire its own living entity.

I gasped. My insides twisting with the revelation that explained so much, and not nearly enough, all at once.

The voices halted, the charge in the air shifting as both men realized I was there. My vision blurred with unshed tears, accompanied by a red hue. Anger and hurt danced together at the prospect that what I'd heard could possibly make sense. The warmth of Hunter's hands suddenly cradling my face, his breath caressing my skin, did wonders to calm the impending panic attack.

"Hey, Sassy. Look at me."

I only then realized my eyes had closed, turning the gray world into black, blinding me to the silent chaos around me. When Hunter repeated himself, I took in a deep breath and lifted my lids to reveal his strong, unyielding face. His worried eyes bored deep into me, reading my emotions like isolated notes on sheet music. One lone tear slid from the inside corner of my eye, running along the side of my nose to fall helplessly onto my lips and coat the seam with salty sadness.

"I heard music," I whispered, my need to ignore Samael's words luring me back to my previous, mortal MO.

"Mara, that's amazing," but his eyes belied his joyful words. This was it. He knew what this meant. I had reached my conclusion, therefore sealing the deal of my accommodations for the rest of eternity.

"No, it's not." He didn't deny my murmured words. Because he knew.

"Mara, what...how much did you hear?" His thumb rubbed a small path beneath my eyes, smearing the wetness from my tear before he lowered his mouth to my forehead.

"Enough." The pit of my stomach felt as though I had been binge drinking for an entire weekend and it was finally time to give my body some rest.

"Let's go to your room," he quietly demanded, but I stayed planted where I stood.

"No. I need to speak with Ernest. I need to tell him." Lifting my gaze to his, I channeled the old Mara. The ever-familiar mask dropped over my eyes, the fake smile opened up like a curtain of survival.

"Don't do that, Mara. Do not hide yourself from me, it won't work." Hunter took a step back and placed his strong, long fingers on my shoulders, and squeezed enough to get my attention.

"I'm not doing anything, Hunter." *Lie.*

"Dammit, Mara. Don't you dare play this game with me. I know you. I've known you for a long fucking time, your walls and armors are not new to me."

I blinked, trying to understand. I knew time was of no relevance here but still. I wouldn't say we had known each other that long.

"That makes no sense, Hunter," I said, trying to push my way around him to get to the library.

"Mara." My name was but a whisper blowing out from between his full, kissable lips. I should have been asking for answers. Any normal, sane person would have been grilling Hunter about his conversation with Samael, but I didn't want to do it. There was no doubt in my mind that whatever those words entailed, it would be more destructive than anything I had endured in my living years.

For interminable seconds, we stood there in the hall staring at each other. Pain etched on his strong facial features, questions lacing my thoughts, we had a wordless conversation.

'We need to talk.'

'I don't want to know.'

'You have to listen.'

'I can't.'

"I need to go, Hunter. I have to talk to Ernest." Our eyes still locked, Hunter released my shoulders and slid his steady hands down the length of my arms until he reached my shaking fingers, squeezing them. My breath hitched at the intimate position we held, my mouth slightly parting to catch my shaky breath.

"I need to talk to you when you get back. Okay?" Hunter's words were mere breaths caressing my cheek as he leaned in and softly dragged his lips across my skin until he reached my mouth. He didn't kiss me, not in that immediate moment. Instead, he glided against my lips, teasing my flesh with barely guarded restraint.

From our proximity, I could feel every beat of his heart as though I were pressed firmly against him.

"Hunter..."

"Shh, just feel me, Mara. Close your eyes and feel me," he whispered.

Releasing one hand, he reached up to the nape of my neck and angled my head just enough for him to perfectly align his lips to mine. Instinctively, I opened for him, allowing his tongue to invade me. I didn't fight him. I didn't want to. I merely let him lead the dance of seduction and allowed myself a minute of pure, adulterated adoration. Words weren't necessary when our body language spoke eloquently enough to have a perfectly discernible conversation. We told each other of our desires. We apologized for past transgressions, whatever they may have been. We spoke of futures we would never have a chance to experience. We said goodbye before our bodies had the chance to ever meet.

Our kiss tapered off to a soft ending, a rallentando eased into a diminuendo, our lips still touching lightly when I heard the clearing of a throat. Hunter groaned before he cupped my cheek in one hand, while the other squeezed my fingers in reassurance, giving me one last lingering kiss.

"I'm all for a little voyeurism but that was just a little too sweet for my tastes. Hunter, let the little lady speak to Papa Smurf and we can finish our conversation," Samael stated, a smirk firmly planted on his mouth, looking pointedly at me. "In private," he added with a little wink.

"I'll see you later, Hunter," I whispered, a little wary of Samael and his plotting eyes.

Taking a step toward Samael, I stopped just inches from his perfectly put-together self, and looked straight into the dark irises of his eyes.

"I can't really be sure, Samael. But I don't think I like you." Without giving him a chance to respond, I walked away, straight to the bookless library.

"I knew there was a reason I liked this one." Samael's deep laughter echoed behind me, his words sending a chill straight down my spine.

12

"Mara, it's good to see you. How is your soul-searching going?" Ernest was difficult to describe, but he had this fatherly quality to him that begged equal parts respect and blinding trust.

"I think I had an epiphany…or something." I took a seat in my usual spot and looked around the familiar room. My eyes caught on another book that had not been there before. Snapping my gaze to Ernest's awaiting eyes, I asked, "Is that for me?"

"Yes, it is. Before you tell me about your revelation, I want you to read the story. It's important." We locked eyes, and I saw the sincerity in his soulful regard.

"Okay," I relented, knowing it was in my best interest to have all of the facts before condemning myself to an eternity of roaring fires and sulfuric smells. Of course, I couldn't be sure that Hell would actually be what everyone claimed it to be. After all, no one had gone and come back to tell stories about it.

"What's Hell like?" My words were barely audible, as though I were afraid the devil himself would hear me.

"It's no place you want to be, Mara."

"Obviously, but, I mean, what's it like? Are we talking lava and demons eating the flesh of the newbies?" I visibly shuddered at the mental images that flashed in my mind.

With a sigh of resignation, Ernest placed his elbows on the table and steepled his hands in front of his mouth as though he were praying to his boss to give him strength.

Yeah, pops, I have that effect on people.

"Below is a mixture of every potent emotion and yet complete nothingness all at the same time. It's your worst nightmare on repeat and your greatest desire just out of reach. It's the constant reminder that your free will is to blame. So, Mara, I'm asking, for your own well-being, to read that book, there." His eyes darted to the lone book on the side and then swung back to me with high expectations.

Standing on admittedly shaky limbs, I made my

way to the far end of the bookshelf and slid an index finger on the spine of the leather binding.

I tilted my head to read the words eloquently written down the length of the book, 'The Ties that Bind'.

"Whose book is..." When I turned to ask Ernest the question, I saw he had already disappeared. It was frustrating how they all seemed to do that. Like ghosts, they came and went silently without warning or preamble.

"Goodbye to you, too, Celestial Freud." My words were mumbled, I barely heard them myself, but felt guilty nonetheless at my smart mouth mocking someone as kind as Ernest, but damn, that beard and those all-knowing eyes, I just couldn't help myself.

Turning my attention back to the task at hand, I tilted the book down and slid it from the shelf.

On the front cover, in small cursive print, was the name of the person whose experiences were contained within.

Sophie Connors aka Sophie Merritt.

She got married? To Jake Merritt? How long have I been here?

Opening the leather cover, I walked distractedly to my usual seat and got comfortable; tucking my feet under me as though readying myself to dive into a Stephen King horror novel.

∞

Two months earlier
Age: Non-documented
Scribe: The Pen of Sceedie
Sophie Connors sat unmoving at the piano that reigned in the center of her childhood home. Her mind, her thoughts, her every emotion an open wound, seconds away from welcoming the inevitable infection of life's dreaded moments.

The pain was unbearable. The guilt, an assassin.

She longed for numbness, a distraction from the reality that her best friend had abandoned her.

That was the pain.

The anger she felt at the betrayal of having to see her best friend's lifeless body had her very bones shaking with reined in violence.

That was the guilt.

Sophie's rational brain knew her actions had not warranted Mara's desire to end her life. But her traitorous heart reminded her every second of her stupidity. A difference of opinion, friends had them every day, but for Mara, it took monstrous proportions. An anthill became Mt. Everest, and a disagreement became a life lost.

Why had she destroyed all their hard work? Sophie could have just taken a calming breath and tried talking sense into Mara the next day. Just one breath. One second to remember the consequences.

She could have just walked away.

Why hadn't she been more present? Instead of spending endless hours falling in love with Jake, she should have been with Mara, should have explained her feeling well enough to make her understand. She should have checked Mara's medication. She should have been there in the place of whatever loser Mara was leaning on for support.

It was her fault. They'd had a pact, with Lucas: Keep her alive, keep her stable.

She'd failed.

And now, Mara was gone.

Sliding her delicate fingers across the ivory keys, Sophie thought of Mara's pale face; her beautiful, sometimes expressive eyes hidden behind closed lids. Her plump, rosy lips hidden behind the blue hue of death.

Black and white keys melted into a blur of nothingness as the tears raced to her eyes, but she fought their descent. Anger was easier to manage. Succumbing to pain would likely destroy her.

Raising her hands in the air, a foot above the ivory, she put all of her strength behind her assault.

"I hate you. I hate you. I hate you." The screams echoed off the walls, running a full circle around the room before returning to her ears and angering her all over again.

"I hate. I hate. I hate!" Mara wasn't the only reason Sophie was angry.

Lucas with his secrets.

Jake with...everything.

Her mother with her indifference.

Society with its ability to destroy the souls within.

Herself, for having her head buried too deep in the sand.

"Hate. Hate. Hate!" Her fingers made no music, only violent, thunderous sounds that amounted to nothing. Just like life. It was all meaningless. It was just a ruse. All of it.

Her phone rang but she just let it go. The noise could just melt into the already existing ruckus of her home.

Maybe she should give up, too?

Everyone else around had, why not her?

What was the point anyway?

Her fingers turned to fists as she pounded away at Mara's favorite instrument, unleashing the powerful ire that threatened to destroy her very sanity.

No.

She wouldn't be that weak. She wouldn't be that selfish.

Sophie would fight back.

Ignore Lucas.

Dismiss Jake.

Forget music.

Hate, hate, hate, Mara.

Except she loved her. More than all of the others.

With one last beating on the keys, she rose to her feet and shuffled away to her room, straight to the bathroom where Mara would surely arrive, ready to braid her hair.

She never did.

The next morning, she woke up in her bed, half dressed with make-up caking her eyes closed and tear-induced snot clogging up her airways.

About to stretch and start her day anew, Sophie stopped and realized two things.

Jake would be a part of her past.

Mara was still dead.

Burying her head back under her covers, Sophie decided life could wait. Numbness took precedence.

13

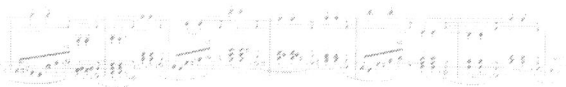

I was crying.
    Sobbing, really.

I had spent so much time bottling up my emotions while alive, that this vulnerability, these tears were frustrating and yet liberating all at once.

Wet stains dotted the relatively new pages of the book as my tears cascaded relentlessly down my cheeks. Of course, I knew my untimely death would upset her; I wasn't completely clueless to the meaning of our friendship. To be perfectly honest with myself, it was my plan all along. A last "fuck you" thrown her way to make sure she felt guilty for her blatant disrespect.

I wanted a reaction from Sophie, for her to acknowledge the depth of her betrayal. I wanted to be the center of the drama, not a sideline spectator. I wanted all eyes on me. Only me. For the world to look at my demise and hang their heads in sorrow and unrelenting grief.

Raising my head, I looked around the gray room, taking in the minimal decoration and utter coldness of the library. Logically, it should have been a place filled with stories and diversions when in reality it was just four walls of despair.

Just like me.

No, correction....

Just like I *used to* be.

I wasn't in agony anymore. The soulless abyss of self-deprecation didn't consume me as it did when I had first arrived. My questions now had answers even if those meant the rest of eternity in the bowels of the Inferno.

I had finally come to a conclusion. I killed myself. I committed suicide and by definition, my place would never be in solace.

My resolution was a welcomed guest.

"Mara?" I turned around so fast, I almost got whiplash. The intruder's voice had invaded my private moment of self-loathing, and publicly displaying my tears had never been a comfortable situation for me.

My nose scrunched up, trying to figure out who the

man before me could possibly be. He was faintly familiar; tall and lean, with proud shoulders ready to carry the weight of the world. Standing at the entrance of the door looking as though he owned it, the handsome intruder cocked his head to the side and took in my appearance. Blue irises so captivating, they almost took my breath away. My eyes travelled along the lines of his perfectly chiseled face, his parted lips mirroring the confusion I felt inside. When our eyes met, I could feel sorrow so deep in the mesmerizing shades of deeply troubled sky, that it threw me for a loop. His pain reflected my own and I hated it.

But as my gaze travelled over the perfect golden locks of his hair, it dawned on me.

Jumping from my seat, book in hand, I did a mental run down of all the information I had on him until I reached his age. Thirty-eight.

No.

Gasping, I shook my head as my feet led me straight to him, the man that should be consoling my best friend.

"Jake Merritt?"

14

"Jake Merritt?" I asked, although the answer was evident and painful all at once.

The man nodded absently as his eyes scanned the room with meticulous precision.

"Wh...What are you doing here?" He wasn't supposed to be here. He was meant to be at Sophie's side, right? The book had Sophie's name. Merritt. It was clear as day.

Looking down at my hands, I verified what I already knew to be true. It did, in fact, have his name as her own.

"Apparently, it would seem I have died." My gasp actually hurt my heart. I was supposed to be dead, how could it hurt so badly?

"No. No, no, no. You can't do that. How? You have

to go back, Jake!" I was rambling, desperately trying to make sense of this impossible clusterfuck. "Sophie won't survive losing you, too. I knew it from the moment she met you. She was in love with you. This will kill her. You can't do that." He had to go back. There was no other choice. Something had to be done.

At first, his eyes swung back to me and the pain raged inside of him. Determination to do the right thing, and then, a moment of abandonment. He was giving up.

Fuck that.

Quicker than I thought possible, I jumped the two steps separating us and pushed him out the door. My ire a palpable, raging fire that surrounded me and gave me the strength I needed to get him moving.

"What are you doing, Mara?" He tried to push me away, but he was losing his footing. It didn't stop him from chuckling at my tantrum.

"You have to go back. You have to go back." I had only one goal in my mind. Maybe there was elevator that would drop him back into his body?

Why hadn't I thought of that? I could have gone back. Truth was, Hunter was here, and it never occurred to me to ever go back to my life. I had no desire to leave.

That singular thought immediately paralyzed me.

"Wait! You want to go back, right?" His answer

would define my entire knowledge of the world and of love.

"Is that a serious question, Mara?" His icy blues bore daggers at me, as though the thought of leaving Sophie willingly was the most absurd concept imaginable.

Nodding, I looked around, trying to find some type of exit sign or a road sign indicating the path back down to Earth. There had to be a way. Didn't Google Maps get service up here?

"What happened? Why are you here?" I asked him, trying to make sense of this whole fucked up mess.

Jake placed his hands on his hips and hung his head in resignation which was not okay.

Not. Okay.

"My heart. One minute I'm arguing with Sophie about us needing to get married and the next I'm here." Running his fingers through his already disheveled hair, Jake exhaled a loud gust of broken breaths. "She's strong, she'll be okay," he finally added.

My temper exploded. The protective part of me refused to let this happen. Sophie's life had never been easy, and losing me probably did quite a number on her. That shit was on me.

But losing Jake? No. Just no.

No matter how strong we both thought she was, this

would annihilate her spirit. Her music would suffer if she even decided to pursue it after this. I couldn't let that happen.

"So, what? You're just going to stand here and let her wilt away? You're not going to fight to get back?" I was pissed. This was not the ruthless man I had researched late at night in the name of protecting my best friend. This was not the man who took what he wanted with no apologies. This was not the man who deserved a woman as strong and independent and fierce as Sophie.

The irony of my own actions did not escape me.

"What the fuck do you suggest I do, Mara? And you're one to talk. You fucking left her willingly. Of your own fucking choice. That woman was the only reason I got up in the morning with a smile on my face. She was my reason for living. I did not go of my own free will." He was right, of course. I was guilty of hypocrisy. "Take me. Save him, and take me."

I barely heard the words, but I recognized Sophie's voice immediately. It was a cry filled with agony and a plead filled with despair. Torment and anguish travelled so far from there to here, that not only could I hear it, but I could feel in my soul. The pain she felt was unbearable. She wouldn't survive it.

"We need to find a way to get you back, Jake. I can't

live with the knowledge that you're here and she's down there, alone." Again with the fucking crying. I was a regular weeping fountain these days.

Shaking his head, the brilliance in his eyes was testament to his overwhelming emotions converted into brimming, unshed tears. He was a beautiful man, passion resonating throughout his entire body, but the truth of the matter was that he had no clue how shit worked up here. I didn't know much more but I couldn't just let this go. I had to do something. Anything.

"I'll find a way, Jake. I just..." I blinked, letting the wet trails cascade down my cheeks and over the seam of my lips; the saltiness filling my mouth. "I just need you to promise me something. If you go back, please tell Sophie I love her. That I'm sorry. I was selfish, but in my heart I knew she was the best friend anyone could possibly have. Can you do that for me?"

I watched him carefully. His determination growing with every word that came from my mouth. His spine straightening with every conviction that grew within him.

"Yes. I promise you." When he chuckled, I was surprised to see myself smiling. "She might think I'm completely crazy but that's a small price to pay if it means holding her in my arms again." His words only solidified my desire to get him back where he belonged.

Looking around, all I saw was gray. The walls, the floors, the ceiling. I had no idea what to do. None.

The past however many days or months I had been in Purgatory flashed in my mind's eye like a film reel, exposing every possibility, every morsel of information that could possibly be useful for this unfathomable situation.

Hunter. Samael. Ernest.

Ernest.

A memory came to me. He'd once said that no one who came in contact with him could go back to life. Maybe...just maybe, Jake could go back before he came face to face with Ernest.

I needed to find him, first. Tell him there was a mistake. Convince him that Sophie was good, and God was good, so the logical solution to the equation would be to bring Jake back to her. Bargain with him. My eternity for hers. It made so much sense, I knew I was destined for Hell anyway, but I had to try. I gave up once, I would never do so again.

Before I knew what I was doing, I looked at Jake and ordered him to "Stay put. Do not leave this spot for any reason until I get back!" Without wasting a second, I turned back to the library, shut the door for good measure, and called out for Ernest.

Within seconds, Ernest was sitting at his desk, his

hands steepled with his fingers resting against his lips. The picture-perfect image of a worried grandfather, ready to help one of his ailing children.

"Oh, thank God! Ernest, I...Look. I have made so many mistakes. I know this." The words were spilling from my mouth a million miles a second, leaving no room for interruptions. I didn't have time for that. He needed to know everything. For the first time in my life, I vowed to be an open book.

For Sophie.

For love.

For friendship.

"Jake has to go back. It cannot be his time. Sophie...she needs him, and I need her to be happy. I broke her, and it's my responsibility to put her pieces back together by giving Jake back to her. Please, Ernest. I'll do anything. I'll be Satan's secretary if he needs one. I'll live in Purgatory forever as a tour guide, if that's what you want. I'm pretty, I could pull off the nice girl. I've never really tried it on for size, but for Sophie? I'd do anything. I promise. I could even spend eternity as a fallen angel and devote myself to souls who need guidance. I've learned from my selfish mistakes, I have. Hunter is a great teacher. Please, Ernest. Anything. I'll do anything God believes I must do. Just...take Jake back to Sophie. Give her back her life in exchange for mine."

I was out of breath after that rant. My chest rose and fell with every breath I labored inside my lungs. I didn't know what else to add, the prospect of not succeeding scared the crap out of me.

"Have you heard music, Mara?"

After all of my pleas and promises, these were the first words he said to me.

Imagine my frustration.

"Wh-? Did you not listen to what I just said?"

"I did. Every single rushed word. Please, answer my question, Mara."

"Ah..." I shook my head, trying to remember if I had, indeed, heard anything, when Nina Simone's raspy voice flitted through my mind. "Yes! Not long ago, in fact. I came here to tell you about my revelation. Not only did I hear music, but I basked in the sounds of an entire song."

"Good. Good. We're happy to hear that, Mara. Very pleased, indeed. Go back to your room, I'll take your request, unorthodox as it may be, into consideration. God and I will discuss the possibilities."

And then he was gone.

Spinning around the room, confirming I was alone, brought about a sinking feeling in my gut. Too much time had passed, right? How long before the soul is permanently detached from the physical body? Maybe I should have specified that Jake needed to go back whole and not comatose for the rest of his life.

Panic grew once more. The inevitable need to lash out, grew from within me, starting at the pit of my stomach and radiating outward toward my extremities. It all begged to come out. Explode.

So, I began screaming.

The frustration of the moment making me completely delirious. The anger and the fear pouring out of me like hot lava bursting from a century-old volcano.

My arms shot straight out on either side of me, my head swung back, and my mouth opened with a roar of resentment. Hunter's name thundered in the surrounding space, the force of my voice surprising even myself.

I hadn't even repeated myself when I felt his all-consuming presence in front of me, his hands on my face trying to calm me.

"Sassy. Hey! Calm down." The soothing voice spoke to me. Calmed my agony, my anger.

"He has to go back. Please," I begged, ready to throw myself at the feet of our Maker, do anything.

"Who, Sassy? Who has to go back?" Hunter looked around, confused.

"Jake. Jake Merritt. He has to go back to Sophie. She'll never survive without him. Please, Hunter. Please...Don't let her suffer more than she already has." By this point, I was a sobbing mess of muscle with liquefied limbs that no longer held my weight.

But Hunter did. He wrapped his arms around my waist and gathered me up into his chest like a child.

"He has to go back, Hunter," I mumbled into this perfect man's neck, my tears drenching his skin, as he began walking us back in the direction of the suites.

"Shh, baby. You're okay. I've got you," I heard him whisper, the pain real and evident.

"No, it's not okay. Sophie won't survive." Before we got too far, I lifted my heavy head to look at Jake but he no longer stood where I had left him. He was gone. That little fact gave me hope.

At first, I was afraid he had been transferred elsewhere, but my heart beat an extra dance. My belly calmed and my brain stopped hurdling possible scenarios. Jake had gone back to her, I could feel it deep inside of me. I don't know why he'd come to me, but I knew without a doubt that it had been temporary.

Reverently, my body was lowered upon soft sheets, a pillow perfectly cradling my head. Hunter lay beside me, on his side, running his fingers in my hair, across my cheeks to dry to tears, over my lips and down the column of my neck. My eyes, as they often did, were drawn to the band of musical notes adorning his bicep, and in a flash of F-sharps and B-minors, it hit me.

"Chopin. Ballad number one, Opus twenty-three." My words were so quiet, I was surprised when he bent his head and gently kissed my lips with what seemed like relief.

"Yes."

"But, why? Why do you have this on your arm?" I was confused, but seeing the notes was bringing vivid memories of me, as a young girl who had just lost her parents, to surface. It hurt, of course, but not as much as it used to.

"It's…"

I cut him off, the need to explain myself so immense that I couldn't wait.

Tracing my index finger along the first notes on his bicep, closest to the crook of his elbow, I told him the story of this ballad. Chopin's number one, his twenty third opus.

"These notes, right here? This continuous loop? It's the beginning of the ballad, right after the introduction. He repeats it twice in the piece, and each time he gives us a false sense of serenity, teasing us into complaisance. Taking us on a picnic on the shores of a mountain lake all the while a storm is brewing in the distance. You know it's there, but you ignore it. You dance and laugh. You eat and relax looking out into the calming, barely perceptible ripples of the water."

Hunter didn't speak, he didn't move. He simply allowed my demons to slowly evaporate from that tight spot in my chest with every word I spoke. Closing my eyes, I poised my hands in the air as though the keys were perfectly placed beneath the pads of my fingers.

"We think we'll be okay, we take a scenic walk on the beach, ignoring the signs, enjoying the rhythmical lull of the E in bass." My fingers spread across the keys, to replicate the composer's creation.

"We believe we'll beat the rain, we kiss, we embrace, we pray for just one more minute…" My left hand jumped over my right as the tempo only I could hear began its acceleration, my heartbeat following the allegretto, fast but not unreasonably so. The fear and the anxiety of what would inevitably be my fate making my breath come in uneven beats.

"But then it happens, suddenly and without mercy, the sky opens, and the heavens come down in a dramatic flair of water pellets. We run, we scream, but the sounds of thunder have the power to silence us." My fingers, all ten sometimes, recreate the fast pace, the allegro in full force.

"In nine minutes, this piece takes you from peace to

hope to happiness to fear and back again, until it leaves you breathless and panting. Like making love then breaking up only to find each other all over again." I looked up and found Hunter's eyes, his focus solely on me, and bared myself to him, "My entire life is told in those nine minutes."

Silence fell between as Hunter digested my verbal feelings, and I basked in the warmth of his embrace.

"I want to add new musical notes to my arms, Mara. Maybe something less depressing? Like, Mozart? Or the B-52's?"

The smile that spread across my face felt like sunshine on a June morning before the City of Angels awakened.

Happiness. I felt it warming inside of me, swirling like a living, breathing thing. It started at the pit of my stomach, and travelled outward until the very tips of my fingers and toes could feel the ethereal healing. I hadn't felt this level of joy since before my teens when my parents had taken us to the zoo where Willy the Orca was temporarily resettled.

Even though that happiness had only lived a mere second inside me, until I saw the desperation etched all over the poor animal in captivity, I had felt it. It had been real, I now knew, because I could again feel it.

I wanted to live in this feeling, bask in it and swim

within its grasp. I wanted to inhale the summery feeling and never let it go.

"Baby? Are you okay?" Hunter's worried eyes searched my face, probably wondering if I was about to have another meltdown.

"Yes. Oh my God. I am...so fucking good right now!" And I meant it.

"Sassy, you're going to get punished for that. You know that, right?" He chuckled when he saw my over-the-top eye-roll. He'd cursed many times before and he was still here, so I wasn't worried about the repercussions. But then taking the Lord's name in vain was probably frowned upon in these parts.

Sitting down on the plush bed right next to me, Hunter brought his index finger up to my temple and dragged it down my cheek, across my chin, and down the slope of my throat. His Adam's Apple bobbing in a nervous attempt to keep cool.

"You saw Jake, then?" Hunter whispered, his eyes following the tender trail of his finger as it danced between the valley of my breasts. I wanted him to touch me, circle my aching nipples with his mouth, caress them with his tongue. I needed him to fill this emptiness inside me and make me feel the sun burning and scalding.

"Yes. He was here, I know he was." My voice was

breathless, his movements creating a surge of something inexplicable inside me.

"He was. He died but he fought it. His doctors were able to bring him back. I'm guessing you're a little responsible for his will to live." Hunter stopped his journey and swung his eyes back up to me. "Is that what you wanted, too? To go back?"

I had asked myself that very question, and the answer was as clear to me at that moment as it was then.

"No. Not without you," I whispered. It was true. I couldn't see myself living without this beautiful, attentive man.

"Hunter? Touch me. Please." I didn't know where the words came from, but I meant those as well. I wanted a more intimate connection to him. To feel his body soothing my body. His mind fusing with my mind.

What I wasn't expecting was his reaction.

"I can't do that, Mara." His words were like steel, but his body was still orbiting toward mine. I sat up on the bed and stared in disbelief at the one man I believed would never reject me. Had I read it all wrong? Was the attraction, the connection I felt, only one-sided?

"What do you mean? You can't, or you don't want to?" Was I not enough for him? Did he find me lacking?

Was I too skinny? Too drama-queenish? Was my baggage too heavy a burden for him to carry?

Deep down, I knew it wasn't the case. These negative, oppressing thoughts were part of the old Mara, not this new, self-aware version of myself. Yet, the doubt was creeping back. While living in Los Angeles, I never really had difficulties finding a warm body to keep me company. I just could never bring myself to go any further. My mind was always drawn to the flaws, the endless reasons why it wouldn't work, the unrelenting obsession to succeed that took precedence over any type of romantic liaison. The overwhelming feeling that if Mr. Right existed, I would know it within seconds of meeting him. It never happened. At least not down there.

"See? What you're doing right now, that doubt written all over your face. That, right there, is the reason I can't. The reason I won't." His tatted-up arms were crossed, revealing the ropes of muscles that brought his art to life. The musical notes that enveloped his bicep peeking out again, teasing my memory. Was that…?

His words were like knives into my soul, and my armor dropped so suddenly it scared even me. I was in fight or flight mode, and for the first time in my existence, fight was my choice.

"That doubt was there only because you just rejected me, you ass!" Jumping from the bed, I stood up to him, facing him head on in this battle of wills. I couldn't believe I was in between Heaven and Hell fighting about sex with the perfect man.

There I was, living my own version of an eye-rolling scene from a soap opera. The Young and the Dead: Purgatory Edition.

"So, fuck me, Hunter. Take me right now," I repeated my words, feeling emboldened by my newfound revelations. Throwing him a dare. Calling him 'chicken'. Pushing him off the pier. No pun intended.

But I needed a reaction. I needed him to fight for me like Jake fought for another day with Sophie. Hunter was my version of a Merritt, and I'd be damned if I took it lying it down.

Actually, that was exactly how I intended to take him.

"I will never fuck you, Mara. I can't. I'm not built for it. I can only make love to you, but not until you love yourself. Not until you see your worth, because once I claim you as mine, it will be for eternity. Are you ready for that kind of commitment? Because, I am." He growled, his fist beating against his own chest. "I have been ready for over a decade, waiting for you. Watching you destroy yourself and wishing I could put you back together."

My spine stiffened at his words. They made zero sense.

"What do you mean, you've been watching me destroy myself? I've been making some pretty spectacular progress since I've been here," I threw at him, reminding him that the difference between hating myself and being able to look at myself in the mirror without feeling disgusted was a notable step-up.

"Mara Mona Reese, I have been in love with you since the day you turned seventeen. My soul recognized his mate, and has been waiting, watching, and crying through every one of your losses, your wins, and your devastations. Yet, through it all, you're still not ready to accept the unconditional devotion that is mine for you. Until then, we can never be." Right before my eyes, Hunter fell to his knees and begged. "So, please, Mara. I'm pleading with you to set me free from this emotional purgatory and love yourself. Just...see what I see. Accept it, love it, and I promise you I will be here when you do. I will give you every part of me."

With a lingering kiss on the inside of my wrist, Hunter rose to his feet, told me to, "think about it" and walked out the door. Again. Leaving me to reflect on the fate of my self-acceptance.

Except, *fuck this shit*.

Turning toward the mirror, I proudly looked over myself. My golden hair had a spring to it I had never noticed, the slight curls at the ends wrapping around my taut cloth-covered nipples. My slender neck gave me a regal elegance I never felt I owned until now. My lips, they were still swollen from our earlier kiss, the pinkish hue bringing out the soft porcelain tint of my skin. Looking up, I stared at myself in the reflection. Bold, determined dark eyes stared right back at me; taunting, defying, commanding.

"Go to him."

"Tell him."

"Show him."

Any other time, I would have considered myself crazy for actually talking to my mirror image, but then again, I was dead, so a little crazy was probably acceptable.

Worst of all, not only did I talk to myself, I even followed my own advice. With a bright smile adorning my lips, I turned toward the door and chased down my soul mate.

15

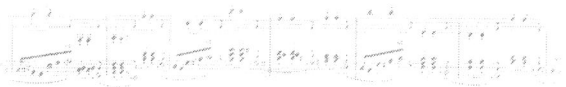

I stormed into Hunter's room like a starving lion chasing down her prey. The tables had turned, I was the huntress, he was mine to do as I pleased. When I threw open the door, the colors around his room assaulted me like an old-school frying pan, knocking me back a couple of steps.

Reds and yellows bled into blues and greens. The bedspread was a dark canary color with a ruby outline that popped the tones beautifully. A painting. A fucking painting, was hanging above his bed. My eyes latched onto it, my heart stopping for a few beats as my brain scrambled to place it in my memories.

It looked like one my mother had done for me when I was younger. An adult hand reaching out to take a child's hand. She had told me that no matter the circumstances, she would always be there to guide me through my life.

This was a replica, the colors were all wrong, and the hand wasn't that of a delicate woman's but that of a strong, protective man. My head snapped to Hunter so quickly, I feared I'd dislodge a couple of vertebrae. There, against the opposite wall, stood my Hunter. My prey. My equal.

"It reminds me of you," was his only explanation. His words from earlier reiterated inside my mind.

"I have been in love with you since the day you turned seventeen."

"I'm ready. I need the truth, all of it. " In warrior mode, ready to take on the facts and leave behind the naiveté, I stood with my legs slightly parted and my arms crossed over my chest.

Hunter's posture was the complete opposite. Leaning against the wall, he tilted his head back and closed his eyes, his mouth slanted down into a frown I wanted to kiss away with my lips. Defeated, almost ready to see me bolt and go.

Where would I go anyway, silly man?

Besides straight to Hell, of course.

"You should sit down, Mara. This might take a while," he murmured, still not making eye contact.

"I'm fine. Go."

And he did.

"I was twenty-six when I died," he began, his voice monotone as though recalling someone else's life story.

"I was in a band, you know? We had just signed a contract with a mid-level label, but still...it was our dream coming to life." Pushing away from the wall, he walked to the bed and sat on the edge, his eyes boring into mine and begging me to join him.

I did.

I uncrossed my arms, anticipating a novel of a story. Slowly, I made my way to him, and instead of sitting beside him, I curled up on his lap. With my head on his shoulder, I wrapped one arm around his waist, and with the other, absentmindedly ran my fingers along his musical tattoo. I listened to the deep timbre of his voice as the vibrations travelled straight to my heart.

"I was driving my heap of an old truck. The tires were barely legal, the breaks needed replacing, and the suspensions were shit. I figured with the cash we were about to earn, I could get a newer model."

He took a deep breath, slightly bending down to kiss my forehead before he resumed his story.

"On my way to my band mates' beat down apartment, I could feel the truck was fucking up on the road. It wasn't far, but I didn't really have a choice. Again, I thought I'd have a new one in less than a week, so I just did my best not to kill myself. Obviously, that didn't work out well."

I wanted to chuckle at his attempt at levity, but I couldn't bring myself to do it.

"Anyway, it started to rain. Like the typical L.A. downpour that lasts about ten minutes and where you can't see shit during that time. I didn't think much of it. I was young and invincible, right? Up ahead, I saw headlights coming, but they were on my lane, sliding at an awkward angle. I tried to stop but my brakes failed. My instinct had me pulling the steering wheel away from the incoming car which isn't what I should have done. Go with the slide, I was always told." Hunter took a little pause, a breath for courage, and gave me the final blow.

"My truck spun out of control and as I flew over the cliff, I felt everything move in slow motion. The other car slammed into the rocks on their side, violently."

When he stopped and didn't start back up, I lifted my head and looked at him, pleading.

"Tell me the rest, Hunter. I know there's more," I begged.

Reaching up, he pushed his thumb into my chin and slanted my head to perfectly align our mouths. His kiss was possessive and supplicating all at once. Rising to my knees, I straddled him, my forearms resting on his strong shoulders; our mouths dancing with pent up emotions we hadn't yet admitted nor ignored. Between each exploration of his tongue, he pulled back nipping and biting at my lips, owning me with his passion.

I hadn't seen Hunter dressed in anything other than his jeans and V-neck shirt, but at that moment, I knew I'd get to see him. Naked. Vulnerable. Mine.

In a move worthy of a porn star, I reached down to the hem of his shirt and pulled it up in one swift move, breaking away from his kiss only long enough to allow the material to disappear. I took a moment to admire the raw, sensual beauty of his naked skin. The ink was perfectly designed, the tribal art, a testament to something a twenty-something, aspiring rock star would have tattooed. It was bold and made his lean muscles pop out even more. His arms, his shoulders, and his pecks all adorned with some kind of ink. I loved the contrast, it made me want him that much more. Hunter's hands moved from my face to my hair, twining it between his fingers and pulling us apart.

"Stop. Look at me," he demanded. I obliged. I stared straight at him, my gaze unfaltering.

"I love you, Mara. Do you hear me?" He was deadly serious, not an ounce of the carefree man I had first met.

"I do. I hear you loud and clear, and Hunter?" I

waited for him to acknowledge my incoming declaration. "I deserve to be loved. I am worthy of colors and music. I have earned the warm feeling of happiness that flutters inside me every time you're close to me. I've made mistakes but I'm a good person." Biting my bottom lip, I hoped my admission would be enough to convince him of my newfound revelation.

"Mara..." There was awe in his voice. It was addictive, that type of reverence.

"Wait. Let me finish." Popping an eyebrow to show my sass, he chuckled and nodded for me to continue. "I was a mess down there. I was sick, I think. I needed to be loved unconditionally and what I missed all that time was that I was loved. By Lucas, by Sophie. By my parents. I thought I needed to be worshipped for my art. My music was everything to me, the perfection of it was my consolation. I could control music. People? Not so much."

"Mara, wait. I have to tell you..." Placing a finger on his lips, I shushed him and smiled.

"When I walked out onto that pier, I did it out of spite. I wanted to punish Sophie for being so fucking perfect. She had the voice, the men, the talent, and the poise to become a star. I was the awkward weirdo at the piano barely able to look at the public, so lost in my notes and keys that outside forces weren't even on my radar. People who couldn't help us make it in the business served no interest to me. Time was precious, and useless company was a waste of energy. I was a mess, Hunter. So, yeah...I walked off that pier and jumped into the ocean of my own free will."

"No, Mara. You were..." He stopped, took a breath and then blew my mind away. "It was Samael. It wasn't you."

We sat there, staring at each other, the silence thickening like the well-known smog of the city. Finally, I asked him to elaborate, because none of his words were making sense to me.

"Samael isn't the Devil or Shaytan. He summons death when a person's time has come. He came for you, Mara. Your desire to walk off the pier was based on his whisperings in your ear." I knew I should have been pissed off. Maybe kicking and screaming and blaming. That's what the old Mara would have done. She would have stormed out and hunted Samael down to rip him a new asshole.

But this Mara, this Sassy, was done. She was done wasting her life or in this case, her eternity.

I stood, feeling bereft of the heat I'd come to associate with Hunter. I stripped my non-descript clothes off me, and presented my naked body to Hunter as a gift.

"I hope God isn't going to send me to Hell for this," I murmured as I took a step toward him, reaching out for his hand and placing it on my stomach; palm open and pressing into my flesh.

"No," he rasped. "He created us with the idea that we could keep each other happy. Sex isn't a sin, Mara. It's the reward for our existence. He wanted us to feel pleasure. It's His gift to us."

Kneeling at his feet, I looked up at his darkening pupils, the deep pools of his irises pulling me in like a whirlwind.

"Are you an angel, Hunter?" I asked him as I lowered my head to his lap. My hands travelled slowly up his thighs all the while I peppered kisses on the inside of his jean-clad thigh.

"Yes," he whispered, his breath catching as one of my hands slid to his zipper, popping the button. Our gazes caught. The air crackling from the hunger growing between us.

"Are you *my* angel, Hunter?" I continued, needing answers but also craving his touch. His bare, naked skin.

"Yes."

"Take your jeans off," I commanded.

Hunter made quick work of his zipper, slipping out

of his jeans. We were both naked, in Purgatory, exploring each other's bodies.

Towering over my kneeling form, Hunter looked down on me with such barely restrained desire that I felt as though I held all the power. Looking in from the outside, I probably seemed submissive, but that picture would be deceiving. I had the control, and I loved it.

"Give yourself to me, Hunter."

With a deep-rooted groan, Hunter took one step closer. One hand latched onto my hair, the other palmed his proud shaft; the thick head weeping with anticipation. In a sensual move that had me shivering with need, Hunter angled his cock to my mouth and circled my lips, painting them with his cum. My tongue darted out in search of his essence, wanting it inside of me.

"Open."

I did as he commanded, my tongue hanging out like a sacrificial offering.

"Do you have any idea how many times I have pictured you this way? Naked and willingly giving yourself to me." Every move was with purpose. His eyes transfixed by the soft connection between my lips and his cock. His hand firmly guiding, round and round, until he used his free hand on my chin to open my mouth wide.

"You are so incredibly beautiful, Mara."

I had never heard another man speak to me with such awe in his voice. It was humbling, and it made my insides tremble with gratitude.

"Every time you hurt yourself," he began, slowly pushing the head of his cock inside my eager mouth. "Every time you gave yourself to another," he continued, tracing the skin where we were joined with the pad of his forefinger. "Every time you cried when the poor bastard left your bed," he gritted through clenched teeth, pushing deeper inside. "Every time you hurt, I died a little more inside."

His words were killing me yet bringing me back to life. Never once, had I felt this loved and wanted in equal measure. I knew lust and its benefits, but I knew nothing of love and its rewards.

Kneeling at his feet, legs slightly apart, fingers digging into his thighs, and my head thrown back with his cock slowly sliding in and out between my lips; I finally understood the almighty high of being in power.

It was heady and I never wanted to lose that feeling.

"Know this, Mara. Once our bodies mate, our souls will become one forever. No turning back now, angel."

As Hunter pulled back, the slick slide of his cock, all rigid and veiny, turned me on beyond anything I had ever experienced.

Before he could push back inside, I asked one last question, "Why are you *my* angel, Hunter?"

I barely had the time to take a breath before his beautiful cock was back inside my mouth. With a tilt of his hips, he buried himself deep inside my throat; my lips touching his pelvis. I was practically choking, his dick invading my entire mouth. Just when I thought I would gag and cough, he pulled out gently, looking down at me with awe.

"To protect you, Mara. It was my responsibility to keep you safe," he answered on a gasp.

"Why you?" I prodded.

He repeated his actions. Fucking me deep down my throat before pulling out again. His control was impressive. The groans that spilled from deep inside his chest were erotic and I wanted more.

"Because it was my absolution."

His words had me frozen, my brows slanted in confusion.

"Stand up, Mara." Pulling me up by the back of my head where his hand had never wavered.

I followed his movements, lifting myself up on shaky legs.

"The car I told you about? It was your parents. I died that night but so did they."

Those damn tears overflowed once again, and

Hunter bent down to kiss them away. Skilled hands caressed every part of my naked flesh, his whispers of apology blew over my skin and seeped into my soul.

This was closure.

Blessed closure.

I had assumed some drunken idiot had taken them away. But no, it *was* an accident. Nothing more, nothing less.

"Kiss me, Hunter. Heal me with your touch."

Bending at the knees, Hunter lifted me into his arms and as our mouths fused with unleashed passion. His cock was nestled tightly against my abdomen, but I wanted him elsewhere. I wanted him inside of me. I needed him to be one with me.

"Hunter, please. I need..."

"What do you need, Mara?"

"You. All of you. Always."

"For eternity, baby. You and me. For eternity," he repeated before bruising my lips with his hunger.

He let himself fall on the bed, his back hitting the down comforter, and his arms locked around me as though holding a priceless treasure. We laughed, our moods in complete contrast with the heavy subjects of conversation.

But for the first time in my existence, I felt light. I

felt I could breathe and not drown. I finally felt like a living being.

How ironic that it was in death that I would finally find life.

"Hunter?"

"Yeah, Sassy?"

"I love you."

"I know."

I burst out laughing, my head thrown back. When I looked back down at my soul mate, he was staring at me with so many emotions swimming in his eyes that I felt the sudden stirrings of ravenous desire.

"Take me, Hunter. Please," I begged him, my mouth sliding across his with the movement of my words.

Large hands lifted me by the waist, and mere seconds later, Hunter was pushing inside of me. His entire being sliding down the walls of my slick pussy. My hands fell to either side of his head as my knees trapped his hips. We stilled, our bodies fusing into one entity. Our gazes locked and our breaths mingling with each exhale.

"You feel so perfect, Mara. Just like I knew you would." His words were a balm to my soul.

"I never thought it could be this powerful. This pure." With a sharp rock of his hips, Hunter pushed further inside, burying himself deeper than I thought possible.

"Yes. Please, yes," I cajoled, my hips meeting his rhythm, thrust for thrust.

Sliding his hands up my back and onto my shoulders, he twisted himself up and over, and in an instant, I was on my back looking up at the most enthralling man I had ever met.

His mouth crashed to mine again, his hips giving me sharp, deep thrusts and hitting my sweet spot over and over again. We were both panting, nirvana just out of reach but closing in on us at a fast pace.

When Hunter's mouth left mine, my lips parted in a silent cry for more.

Raining open-mouthed kisses down the length of my neck, he gently bit the flesh until he reached my aching breast. His tongue circled my erect nipple before taking it deep into his mouth and opening a direct line to my clenching pussy.

"We're two pieces of one puzzle, Mara, and together we create the big picture. Can you feel it? "

My hands dove into his messy hair, and I held on for dear life as he devoured every inch of my skin available to him. His body was a vessel of carnal need, but his mouth was a direct source of love.

He was consuming me and giving me everything he had.

He was fusing our souls and holding nothing back.

"Oh, Hunter!"

"Come for me, angel. Come all over me." His command wrapped in a plea was my undoing. My entire body gave up the fight. The walls of my pussy tightened so forcefully, I was afraid I would hurt him. But with his hands buried in my hair and his mouth attacking mine anew, we both let ourselves go into a tornado of bliss, and a rollercoaster of emotions.

We cried out in ecstasy.

We let go of the past.

We embraced our futures.

We both came back to life and gave in to death. On our terms. With our bodies and souls.

We fused.

Forever.

16

HUNTER

Making love to Mara was beyond any fantasy or dream I could have conjured up myself. I had waited so long for us to be together that I never thought it would happen. She was young, she had her entire life to live out among the mortals. I was ready to wait. Had prepared myself for the long years on the sidelines until the fateful day she would pass on to my world.

That day came much sooner than expected. As much as I yearned to make her mine, I wanted her to live a long life, hoped she would be happy despite her rough start.

Lying on my back with Mara's long blonde hair loosely twisted between my fingertips, I let my mind wander to that fateful night. I froze when her breath hitched, her head resting snugly against my chest, her sleepy breaths caressing my heated skin.

I was angry when she, yet again, started sleeping with that douchebag junkie. He was nice enough with her, but he always pushed her to join him with his overdrinking and drugs. I watched, helplessly, as she and Sophie fought, and felt physical pain when at the sight of agony on Mara's face when Sophie put the lighter to the music sheets they'd worked so hard creating.

Then, I stepped in front of her, begging her to turn around as she took the last step off the pier, her blood overrun with alcohol. I screamed at her to back the fuck off. I tried, in vain, to materialize somehow and yank her back. Nothing worked. I dove in the water and accompanied her as she let herself sink, eyes wide open and staring at me without seeing me. She didn't die alone, I was there with her; dying on the inside.

"I can hear you thinking."

I chuckled at her raspy voice, her body stretching like a kitten before falling limp.

"Is that so? What is it I'm thinking, Sassy?"

Her hand slowly slid down the length of my stomach, inching dangerously toward my dick; to his utter delight.

With a grin plastered on my face, I tightened my grip

on Mara's hair and started to bring her beautiful face closer to mine. I wanted to kiss her, taste her in her waking moments, and inhale her sweet scent into my lungs.

Less than a second after I heard the loud double knock, my door burst open and Samael stood at the entrance, his grin a mile wide. Quickly, I covered my girl up with my body as best I could.

"I accept verbal, written, or sexual 'thank yous'," he announced, leaning against the door jamb.

Mara jolted wide awake, hiding herself beneath the down comforter, screeching obscenities his way.

I tried and failed to hide my chuckle, shaking my head at Samael's antics.

"Why would we do that?" I asked.

"Well, first," he began, ticking off his list on his fingers, "I'm responsible for your little love nookie."

"I'm pretty sure I'm responsible for that," I answered. "Now get the fuck out."

"Nah, I've got something I need to say to your little angel."

"You creep me out, Sam," I heard Mara's muffled voice from beneath the covers.

Samael and I both laughed at that. She was right. The Angel of Death was nothing if not creepy.

"Well, I'll have you know, Mara, that I'm only a

creeper down there," he said this while pointing his index finger downward.

"In Hell?" she asked.

"On Earth. Hell isn't all that bad, you know. What with all the partying, drugs, and sex galore." He was so full of shit, it was nauseating.

"Sounds like L.A.," she muttered.

"It's safer than the City of Angels, believe me. The only one causing unwanted pain is Shaytan himself, and no one argues with that crazy fucker."

"Samael, seriously. Get the fuck out."

"Look. I wanted to say something." He straightened his posture, all joking aside. A look of determination etched over his perfectly chiseled face.

"I'm the reason you're here. I spoke with Ernest about it, but that old man already knew." Shaking his head, he lowered his gaze before pinning Mara with an intense gaze.

"I did it for Hunter. And for you. This past decade, he's been pining for you, and your life was going to shit. So, when you started walking to the pier, I put ideas in your head. I whispered sweet nothings of pain disappearing under the water. In my defense, you really didn't take much convincing but still..." Letting his sentence trail off, he shoved his hands inside the pockets of his tailored suit pants and grinned like a ten-year-old waiting for forgiveness.

"I know," she said. "I heard you earlier."

"So...we good?" That little shit, he felt zero guilt. But deep down, I knew he was doing this for me. For her, even. Eternity would be a long time for her to wonder why she had given up so easily. Samael was taking her guilt away and placing it on his shoulders.

Everyone on Earth always gave him a bad name, but Samael had the hardest job of all. Collecting souls was never an easy task. Not even for the evil doers. Every life taken was a piece of Samael that withered away.

For as long as I'd known him, he never got close to anyone because emotions were difficult for him. Of all of us, he was the only one able to travel from Heaven to Hell whenever need be. Collecting and distributing souls was his assigned job and he'd been doing it for eons. It was a heavy burden, and joking, being crude, and all around creepy was his way of lightening up his fucked-up role in this universe.

"How about you get me out of Purgatory and into a permanent home, and I'll forgive you?"

"Deal."

Little did Mara know that Samael had no power in that domain and that decision had probably already been made by Ernest. I was curious as to her assignment.

"Get out, Samael. Leave me alone with my girl, will ya?" Exasperated, I threw a pillow from behind my head and nearly hit my target. The door closed behind him as he threw me a wink over his shoulder.

"We have a meeting in ten, kid. Get your ass dressed."

17

MARA

"Mara. It's nice to see again. You look much better than last we met." Ernest greeted me with grandfatherly eyes that searched my face.

"I feel much better, thank you."

"Good, good." Turning to Samael and Hunter, he directed us all to have a seat in the plush couches strategically placed around a round glass-top coffee table.

We were in Ernest's office, a place I had never seen before. Progress, right?

"Our Lord and I have spoken extensively about Mara's file. We have come to the conclusion that she indeed walked off that pier with ill intent, but not of her own free will," he said this with a pointed look in Sam's direction.

"All in the name of love, Papa Bear," this coming from Samael. How he got away with his antics was beyond me. "Can I get an 'Amen'?" Sam added, with a toothy grin that made a dimple pop out like a beacon.

"We coddle you too much, Samael. Tone it down," Ernest quickly shot back.

"I'll give an 'Amen' to that," added Hunter with a chuckle.

Me? I felt like I was watching a sit-com in an alternate universe.

"All right, settle down before I put you both on sulfur duties." They both visibly shuddered, the threat apparently working like a charm.

Everyone sat down. Ernest directly in front of me, with Hunter to my right, and Samael to my left. Each owning their own demeanor. The wise, the serious and the mischievous.

And then there was me...the clueless.

"Mara. We have decided to give you your wings. Hunter here, will be your mentor and partner."

I blinked, then directed my gaze to Hunter who had a grin so wide on his face I feared it would hurt him.

"Okay," I answered, drawing out the last syllable. "What exactly does that mean?"

"It means, child, that you will be going back to Earth and earning your place in the Heavens. You must help, guide, and better one soul. You will be responsible for their well-being, nudge them in the right direction."

"But...I don't know much about religion. What if I screw up?" Why would anyone make me responsible for another human being? I was barely able to take care of myself.

"Mara, listen to me. Believing in God and believing in religion are two different things. Our Lord loves all of his children. Each of their lives is precious. Their actions are oftentimes guided by ill forces, and your job will be to make sure those forces are for the good of the masses. Those around them."

"So, Hunter was a lousy angel, then?" I bit my lip to avoid laughing.

"Let's say...Hunter was preoccupied. Or to be more accurate, his soul was yearning."

Samael snorted, Hunter blushed. It was endearing because his less than stellar work as my guardian angel was due to his growing love for me.

I could accept that.

As for Sam? He wasn't so bad, I supposed.

After all, he may have driven me to die but he saved my soul in the process.

"So, where will our assignments take place?" Hunter asked, looking at me with a reassuring smile.

"Back to square one, my child. Back to square one."

Ernest's cryptic answer seemed to make sense to both men. Of course, I felt just as confused as ever.

"What does that mean?" I asked, looking at Hunter then Ernest.

"The City of Angels, of course. We believe it is in everyone's best interest that you guard the one that loved you unconditionally."

His answer shocked me. Thrilled me. Had me gasping.

"Lucas?"

"No, Mara. Lucas has Kael watching over him. He's really good too. I'll introduce you as soon as we get down there," Hunter said, reaching out to lace his fingers through mine.

"Which means...Sophie?" My heart soared. The thought of being able to watch her grow and become everything she ever wanted had my soul bursting with joy.

"Yes. Sophie will be your charge. Do you feel capable of such a responsibility?" Ernest asked, his fingers steepled under his chin, his eyes considering every one of my reactions.

"Yes. Of course. That would be amazing."

"Then it's settled. Hunter, you of course, will be taking care of Jake Merritt. Lord knows he needs to be reined in. Make sure he feels the need to redistribute that growing fortune of his. Good thing he's fallen a little farther from his father's tree." Samael chuckled at Ernest's attempt at humor and Hunter joined him. As for me, I didn't know Jake well enough to understand the inside joke.

"Now, go forth and protect the living."

And so, we did.

Epilogue ~ Mara

I watched Sophie sing at her wedding.

It was glorious and sad all at once. Her voice was more beautiful, more powerful than ever.

Hunter stood behind me, his arms wrapped around my waist, my head resting against his chest.

Being a guardian angel wasn't so bad. Of course, being Sophie and Jake's guardian angels wasn't a piece of cake, either. Those two were explosive on a good day, and downright nuclear when things did not go as planned.

I sensed a bit of trouble brewing. Jake's possessive streak and his close call with death had his nails digging into Sophie's need for independence. She'd never had to answer to anyone, really. Her mother was doing her own thing, and her father had died when she was young enough to block out the memory of him. I worried Jake would fuck it all up by saying something ridiculous like "I forbid you…" I knew Sophie, it would send her packing in a heartbeat.

And Lucas…

Watching Lucas grow into his own slow rising success gave me pride. He'd never told me he was bisexual. It hurt, at first. Not being trusted with my twin's inner most turmoil. I never would have judged him. But I've learned to forgive and accept.

As Sophie belted out her last syllable on that stage, wearing a dress that encompassed both her sexiness and her simplicity, Sophie touched every single heart and soul that attended their wedding. She couldn't have seen though because her eyes were fixed on Jake's, her love pouring out from her every pore. And it was reciprocated ten-fold from Jake.

The reception was simple, with only close family and friends, which was no surprise. It was about an hour after she'd uttered the last vowel of her performance that I'd seen her leave Jake's side and heading outside, alone.

I knew I didn't have much time, which meant I needed to extricate myself from Hunter's hold and join my best friend before her possessive husband came running after her.

He never could bear being away from her.

Stepping outside on the balcony, I noticed the single thin braid in Sophie's hair and smiled. It was her way of including me on her big day. Little did she know, I was there. For her. For me. For our friendship. As her hand rose to her braid and her fingers tightened around the dark strands, I knew she was there to think of me, of us, and of all the lost moments we would never share. She often sought out moments of solitude like this, and I was always there to accompany her even if she could never really know.

But on her wedding day, I did what I wasn't supposed to do. I tried to send her my vibe, my love...my presence.

I wanted to let her know that I was okay and that I wanted her to be happy. To live. To succeed like no other.

So, I whispered my wishes and hoped she felt them deep inside.

"I love you, Sophie. Be happy. I'm good and I'll always be here for you. I promise."

I watched her as her gaze rose to the clear night sky above, and a single tear fell from her eyelash and carved a path down her perfectly made-up face. She closed her eyes as I made my promises, and inhaled a deep, fortifying breath before Jake came out and wrapped her up in his large embrace, his mouth at her bare neck.

Hunter was right behind him, shaking his head and rolling his eyes, mirth dancing in his irises.

"I swear, that man lives, breathes, and fucks Sophie Connors. As for the rest, no cares, not one," Hunter told me as Jake explained to Sophie that her name was no longer Connors but Merritt. And as such, he should be able to find her when looking for her.

"Sorry. I mean, Sophie Merritt. I swear, sometimes I think he hears me talking. Like his possessive side goes beyond the realm of mortals," Hunter whispered in my ear.

"It's kinda hot, though. You know?" I responded, watching the way Jake worshipped Sophie with every one of his senses.

"I'll keep that in mind, angel."

"I think we should give them some privacy. It's about to get nuclear out here," I told him, linking my fingers through his and leading him away from our charges.

"Bet I can make you scream louder than her." And that he did. In a room full of people who could not see us, Hunter made me his for eternity.

Again, and again.
Amen.

       That's it…or maybe not.

AFTERWORD

Depression is a silent, invisible disease. I know, I've been there, and it was Hell. For me, for my family, for my friends who all watched powerless as I sank deeper and deeper into walled up abyss. The worst part is knowing you are sinking and having zero energy left in you to fight it off.

For over a year, I pretended I was fine. I smiled at the right times and laughed on cue. I had a colleague tell me I was the sunshine of our establishment because my smile was so bright.

I was dying inside.

Every day, I would cry going to work...put on a smile, get my job done and then get into my car...then I would cry the whole way going home.

One day, the pressure was too much and I broke

down in my boss's office. She told me to go home and I didn't go back to work for over six months.

People around you say things like: "Come on, snap out it." or "But you have everything you need to be happy." These phrases hurt more than they help. Because when you're depressed you know things could be worse, and so hearing it from others makes the guilt even stronger thus plunging you deeper into the dark. That's when you stop accepting calls or responding to messages.

Every time the phone rang, I had panic attacks because it meant people on the outside were trying to communicate, which meant having to be responsible for something. I had nothing to give during that time. Nothing.

I couldn't even force myself to go outside onto my terrace. Imagine that...feeling so oppressed from the outside world that the only place I felt safe was inside my home. Alone. Always alone.

Why am I telling you this? Because if someone around you is going through depression, you need to help them by actually listening to them without judgment. Be there for them even if it's by not physically being there. Try to understand that it's not a choice. We do not choose to ball up in a corner and avoid any contact. It just feels safer that way.

If you are experiencing depression, seek out someone to talk to...if you feel you need it and can actually do it.

How did I get out of it? I started writing.

Writing was my sanctuary and over the course of a few months, I started smiling again, albeit tentatively. I cried less into the night. I quit staying up until five in the morning so I could sleep the next day and avoid contact with anyone.

I started living the day I brought to life my characters.

Find something that is only yours: a sport, an art, gardening...anything that makes you feel something other than despair.

I think this is why I was so attracted to Mara's character. I understood her and I loved her for it.

If you or someone you love is in need of help, please contact your local help center.

US: https://suicidepreventionlifeline.org/

UK: https://www.samaritans.org/

France : https://www.sos-amitie.org/

ACKNOWLEDGMENTS

Although this story was originally a Drazen World story from CD Reiss' The Submission series, I decided to keep these acknowledgements intact because even though I've changed a few things and added others, these sentiments are still valid. Without these ladies, this book wouldn't exist.

…

Writing this book was anything but a piece of cake.

Not the story itself, that was the easy and fun part. But the constant second guessing.

I had originally written this story under the title "Purgatory" for CD Reiss' Kindle World and *that* was no easy feat, the pressure was definitely on.

There are a few ladies I need to thank for making this story come to life.

Kerry Heavens...I love that I can ALWAYS count on you. Thank you!

Jean Siska...your support and input was golden. I could not have done it without out you. Seriously.

Julie Linhart and Lauren Lascola-Lesczynski thank you for putting me on the right path!

My Drazen World Sisters... Kristi Beckhart Book 1- Run and Book 2- Hold, K. Nilsson--Improper, Lauren Luman -- Red Velvet, it's an honor to stand by your side.

Sarah Goodman – Thank you for stepping in to make sure it was all a good to go! You're amazing and am so lucky to have you!

Sloane Murphy – Thank you for keeping my head straight and my words flowing. You are loved and appreciated.

And of course...a huge, warm, fuzzy, wine induced THANK YOU to the Goddess that made it all possible...This one's for you, Christine.

ALSO BY EVA LENOIR

UNDERDOGS OF THE ARENA SERIES

(Paranormal Romance)

Bloodweight

Stone Cold

White Fire

#UCC SAGA

(Contemporary Romance with a dash of RomCom)

Disheveled

Disarmed

Discarded

STANDALONES

(Contemporary Romance)

The Wish

Screwed: A Driven Novel

ABOUT THE AUTHOR

I love nothing more than hearing back from readers. Contact me at eva.lenoir.author@gmail.com or join my private FB group:

Ruby's Lounge http://bit.ly/Rubyslounge
FB: https://bit.ly/EvaLeNoirFB
GR: https://bit.ly/EvaLeNoirGR
Twitter: https://bit.ly/EvaLeNoirTwitter
Instagram: https://bit.ly/EvaLeNoirInstagram
Pinterest: https://bit.ly/EvaLeNoirPinterest
Website: https://bit.ly/EvaLeNoirWebsite
BookBub: https://bit.ly/BookbubEvaLeNoir